W.W Worster

Egholm and His God

outlook

W.W Worster

Egholm and His God

1st Edition | ISBN: 978-3-75234-253-6

Place of Publication: Frankfurt am Main, Germany

Year of Publication: 2020

Outlook Verlag GmbH, Germany.

Reproduction of the original.

Egholm and his God

By W. W. Worster

I

Sivert stands leaning his elbows on the window ledge, digging all ten fingers into his curly hair, and looking down at the muddy court below.

Not a soul.

He looks at the wet roofs, and the raindrops splashing tiny rings in the water all along the gutter.

Not so much as a sparrow in sight. Only the sullen November drizzle, flung now and then into gusts, and whipping the panes with a lash of rain.

But that is enough for Sivert. He looks out into the grey desolation, highly amused at it all.

Now he purses up his lips and whispers something, raises his eyebrows, mutters something in reply, and giggles.

Let him, for Heaven's sake, as long as he can, thinks his mother.

And Sivert finds it more amusing still. Wonderful, so much there is going on inside him. He shakes his poodle mop of hair, and gives way to a long-drawn, gasping laugh—simply can't help it—leans his forehead against the pane, thrusts both hands suddenly deep into his pockets, and gives a curious wriggle.

"You great big boy, what's the matter now?" says his mother gently.

Sivert turns his head away and answers with an evasive laugh:

"All that rain ... it tickles so."

Fru Egholm does not question him again; for a moment she really feels as if the boy were right. And, anyhow, it would be no use asking him. If only he can find his little pleasure in it, so much the better.

And there's no saying how long ... Egholm had said it was time the boy found something to do, now he was confirmed. Find him a place at once. And Sivert, poor weakly lad—how would it go with him?

Fru Egholm shakes her head, and sends a loving glance at the boy, who is plainly busy in his mind with something new and splendid.

Then suddenly his face changes, as if at the touch of death itself. His eyes grow dull, his jaw drops; the childish features with their prematurely aged look are furrowed with dread as he stares down at something below.

"Is it Father?" she whispers breathlessly. "Back already?"

She lays down her sewing and hurries to the window; mother and son stand watching with frightened eyes each movement of the figure below.

Egholm walks up from the gate, lithe and erect, just as in the old days when he came home from the office. But at every step his knees give under him, he stumbles, and his wet cloak hangs uncomfortably about him. At last he comes to a standstill, heedless of the fact that his broad boots are deep in a puddle of water.

Once he looks up, and Sivert and his mother hold their breath. But the flower-pots in the window hide them. His head droops forward, he stands there still. A little after, they see him trudging along close to the wall, past his own door.

The watchers stand on tiptoe, pressing their temples against the cold glass, straining to see what next.

Egholm stops at the Eriksens' gate, glances round, and kneels.

Kneels down full in the mire, while the gale flings the cape of his ulster over his head. Now he snatches off his hat and crushes it in his fingers; his bald head looks queerly oblong, like a pumpkin, seen from above.

"He's praying!"

And the two at the window shudder, as if they were witnessing some dreadful deed.

"Where am I to hide?" blubbers Sivert.

The mother pulls herself together—she must find strength for two.

"You need not hide to-day. Take your little saw and be doing some work. You'll see, it will be all right to-day."

"But suppose he counts the money?"

"Oh, heaven...!"

"Hadn't we better tell him at once? Shout out and tell him as soon as he comes in, and say Hedvig took it?"

"No, no."

"Or go and kill ourselves?"

"No, no. Sit still, Sivert dear, and don't say a word. Maybe God will help us. We might put something over the bowl … no. Better leave it as it is."

Heavy steps on the stairs outside. Egholm walks in, strong and erect again now.

He hangs up his wet things, and fumbles with a pair of sodden cuffs.

"Didn't get a place, I suppose?" asks his wife, looking up from the machine. Sivert sits obediently at a little table at the farther end of the room.

"Is it likely?" Egholm's face is that of one suffering intensely. And he speaks in an injured tone.

"I only thought…. You're home earlier than usual."

No answer. Egholm walks over to the window and stares into the greyness without, his long, thin fingers pulling now and again at his dark beard.

Lost in thought….

His wife does not venture to disturb him, though he is shutting out the fading light. She keeps the machine audibly in motion, making pretence of work.

A long, long time he stands there. Sivert has been sawing away conscientiously all the time, but at last he can bear it no longer, and utters a loud sigh. Fru Egholm reaches stealthily for the matches, and lights the lamp. Her fingers tremble as she lifts the glass.

Egholm turns at the sound. And now he is no longer Egholm the upright, nor Egholm the abject; *Egholm the Great* he is now. His eyes glow like windows in a burning house; he stands there filling the room with Egholm; Egholm the invincible. The mother cowers behind her sewing-machine; and her seam runs somewhat awry.

What terrible thing can he be thinking of now? The "Sect," as usual?— Heaven have mercy on them, now that Egholm has joined the Brotherhood.

Surely something terrible must happen soon; he has rarely been as bad as this before.

He moves, and his wife looks up with a start. But now he has changed again, to something less terrible now—not quite so deadly terrible as before.

He is far away in his dreamings now, without a thought for his earthbound fellow-creatures.

He stands in his favourite attitude, with one hand on his hip, as if posing to a sculptor. A fine figure of a man. His watch-chain hangs in a golden arc from one waistcoat pocket to the other. Only one who knew of the fact would ever notice that one of the oval links is missing, and a piece of string tied in its place.

After a little he begins walking up and down, stopping now and again at the window, with a gesture of the hand, as if addressing an assembly without.

Then suddenly he swings round, facing his wife, and utters these words:

"Now I know what it means. At last!"

Fru Egholm checks the wheel of her machine, and looks up at him with leaden-grey, shadow-fringed eyes. But he says no more, and she sets the machine whirring once more.

Peace for a little while longer, at any rate, she thinks to herself.

Sivert looks up stealthily every time his father turns his back; the boy is flushed with repressed excitement, the tip of his tongue keeps creeping out.

"Mark you," says Egholm after a long pause, "I'm wiser perhaps—a good deal wiser—than you take me for."

He throws out his chest with conscious dignity, lifting his head, and placing one hand on his hip as before.

Oh, so he's still thinking of that quarrel of theirs this morning. Well, well, of course it would be something to do with the Brotherhood some way or other.

"You said I was wasting my time."

"I didn't say that."

"You said I was throwing money out of the window."

Fru Egholm shifts in her seat, pulling nervously at her work. She would like to mitigate the sharpness of her words, and yet, if possible, stand by what she had said.

Sivert wakes to the fact that he is dribbling down over his hand, and sniffs up hastily.

"Didn't you say it was throwing money out of the window?"

"I said, it was hard taking money where there was none."

"You said it was throwing money away. But do you know what I'm doing with that money all the time? I'm putting it in the bank."

"In the bank?..."

"In the *Bank of Heaven*—where the interest is a thousand—nay, tens of thousands—per cent.! If it wasn't for that, I'd never have thought of joining the Brotherhood at all."

"But—I can't help it, but I don't believe in him, that Evangelist man. Young Karlsen, I mean."

Egholm breathed sharply, and quickened his steps. The answer did not please him.

"You talk about young Karlsen: I am talking of Holy Writ."

"But it was Karlsen that...."

"Yes, and I shall thank him for it till my dying day. He it was that opened my eyes, and showed me I was living the life of one accursed; pointed out the goal I can reach—cannot fail to reach—if only I will pay my tithe. Do you know what it says in Malachi? Shall I give you the words of Malachi the Prophet?"

"Ye—es ... if you please," answers his wife confusedly.

"Yes ... if you please," echoes Sivert in precisely the same tone. He has a painful habit of taking up his mother's words when anything excites him.

But Egholm had no time now to punish the interruption; he stood forth and spoke, with threatening sternness:

"'Will a man rob God? Yet ye have robbed me. But ye say, Wherein have we robbed thee? In tithes and offerings.'

"'*Ye are cursed with a curse....*'

"Cursed!" Egholm struck the table with his fist in condemnation. "Do you hear? They are accursed who would rob the Lord—*in tithes and offerings!*"

"It's solemn hard words," said the mother, with a sigh.

"No harder than it should be. Just and right!"

"I was only thinking—the New Testament—perhaps there might be something there to make it easier."

"Make it easier! God's Law to be made easier! Are you utterly lost in sin, woman? Or do you think I would tamper with the Holy Scriptures? Read for yourself—there!"

He snatched the old Bible from its shelf and flung it down on the sewing-machine. Fru Egholm looked at the thick, heavy tome with something like fear in her eyes.

"I only meant ... if it was really God's will that we should starve to find that money for Karlsen."

"Starve—and what's a trifle of starvation when the reward's so much the greater? What does it say there, only a little farther on: '*Prove me now herewith, saith the Lord of Hosts, if I will not open you the windows of heaven, and pour you out a blessing, that there shall not be room enough to receive it*'?

"Isn't that a glorious promise? Perhaps the finest in the whole Bible. Are you so destitute of imagination that you cannot see the Lord opening the windows of heaven, and the money pouring out like a waterfall, like a rainbow, over us poor worms that have not room enough to receive it?"

"Money?—but it doesn't say anything about money."

"Yes, it does—if you read it aright. It's there all right, only"—Egholm drew his lips back a little, baring his teeth—"only, of course, it needs a little sense in one's head to read the Bible, just as any other book. It wasn't all quite easy to me at first, but now I understand it to the full. There's not a shadow of doubt, but the Bible means *ready money*. What else could it be? The blessing of the Lord, you say. Well, there's more than one of the Brethren in the congregation thinks the same—and that's what makes them slow in paying up *their* tithes and offerings. They think the blessing is just something supernatural; an inner feeling of content—fools' nonsense! Do you suppose I could be content, with duns and creditors tearing at me like dogs about a carcase? No; ready money, that's what it means. Money we give, and money shall be given unto us in return; we shall receive our own with usury, as it is written."

"Do you really mean...."

Egholm grasped eagerly at the hint of admission that he fancied lay behind her doubt. He strode to the chest of drawers, and, picking up the crystal bowl, held it out towards the light as if raising it in salutation. The tithe-money showed like some dark wine at the bottom.

"I swear unto you," he said, with great solemnity, "it is even so."

Fru Egholm meets his burning glance, and is confused.

"It would be a grand thing, sure enough, if we could come by a little money." And she sighs.

"But it's not a little," says Egholm. The impression he has made on her is reacting now with added force upon himself. "Not altogether little; no. I can feel it; there is a change about to come. And a change, with me, must be a change for the better. It means I am to be exalted. 'Friend, come up higher!'"

Again he strides up and down, seeking an outlet for his emotion. He sets down the bowl, and picks up the Bible instead, presses the book to his breast, and slaps its wooden cover, shaking out a puff of worm-eaten dust.

"Beautiful book," he says tenderly—"beautiful old book. By thee I live, and am one with thee!" And, turning to his wife, he goes on: "After all, it's simple enough. If I do my duty by God, He's got to do His by me, and I'd like to see how He can get out of it."

There was a rattle of the door below. Fru Egholm listened … yes, it was Hedvig, coming back from her work. There—wiping her boots on Eriksens' mat, the very thing she'd been strictly forbidden. And dashing upstairs three steps at a time and whistling like a boy. No mistaking Hedvig.

Fru Egholm signed covertly to Sivert to go out in the kitchen. She could give the children their food there, without being noticed. What you don't hear you don't fear, as the saying goes. And that was true of Egholm; it always irritated him when Sivert made a noise over his food. Poor child—a good thing he'd the heart to eat and enjoy it.

Hedvig came tumbling in, with a clatter of wooden shoes.

"Puh, what a mess! I'm drenched to the skin. Look!" She ducked forward, sending a stream of water from the brim of her hat. Her hair, in two heavy yellow plaits, slipped round on either side, the ends touching the floor; then with a toss of her head she threw it back, and stood there laughing, in the full glare of the lamp.

Glittering white teeth and golden eyelashes. The freckles round her nose gave a touch of boyishness to her face.

"My dear child, what can we give you to put on?"

"Oh, I'll find some dry stockings—there's a pair of mine in the settee."

"Sivert borrowed those, dear, last Sunday, you know. But you can ask him—he's outside in the kitchen."

Egholm, too, must have his meal. He had a ravenous appetite. The pile of bread and dripping vanished from his plate as a cloud passes from the face of the moon. Possibly because he was reading, as he ate, of the land of Canaan, a land flowing with milk and honey.

The rain spattered unceasingly against the panes.

"What are you hanging about here for?" asked Hedvig. Sivert was standing huddled up by the sink.

"He'll find out in a minute," whispered the boy. "He's waving his arms and legs about, and talking all about money."

"Puh—let him. We must eat, so there's an end of it. He'll have forgotten by to-morrow how much there was."

"But he'll count it to-night. He's going to the meeting."

"To-night—h'm. That's a nasty one," said Hedvig thoughtfully.

Sivert showed a strange reluctance to hand over the stockings.

"They've been confirmed," he explained. "I wore them last Sunday. You can't have them back now after they've been to my confirmation. It's a great honour."

"You take them off, and that sharp! You can see mine are wet through."

"Mine are ... they're wet, too."

"Wet, too? Why, what have you been doing?"

"I—I couldn't help it," snivelled Sivert shamefacedly. "It came of itself, when Father took the bowl...."

Hedvig drew away from him, turning up her nose in disgust.

"Ugh! You baby!"

"Mother! Is she to call me a baby now I'm grown up and confirmed?"

"Hold your noise, out there!" cried his father. "Run down to Eriksens' and ask the time."

Sivert hurried away, and brought back word: half-past seven.

"I must be off," said Egholm, with an air of importance.

Mother and children looked with a shiver of dread towards the cut-glass bowl. But Egholm was quietly putting on his still dripping coat, looking at himself in the glass, as he always did. It was a game of blind man's buff, where all save the blind man know how near the culprit stands.

"Leave out the key, Anna, if I'm not...."

"Oh, I'll be waiting up all right."

"Well, if you like." Egholm moved to the door; he grasped the handle. A flicker of hope went through them; he had forgotten his tithe and offering. To-morrow it wouldn't matter so much....

But Egholm stood there still, pulling at his beard, straining himself to think....

"Ah—I mustn't forget the chiefest of all."

In the midst of a ghastly silence he took the bowl from its place, shook out the little heap of coppers, and with a satisfied air stacked them up in orderly piles, ready to count. He counted all through, counted over again, and moved the piles in different order, pulled at his beard, and glowered. The mother kept her eyes fixed on her work, but the children were staring, staring at their father's hands.

"How much was it he lent us on the clock last time? Three *kroner*, surely?"

"Yes; I think it was three," said Fru Egholm, trying her hardest to speak naturally.

"What do you mean?—'you *think* it was!'" Her husband rose to his feet with a threatening mien.

"Yes, yes, I remember now. It *was* three *kroner*."

"And did you put the thirty-*øre* tithe in the bowl, as I ordered?"

Fru Egholm felt instinctively that it would be best to insist that the money had been put in the bowl. But another and stronger instinct led her at this most unfortunate moment to hold forth in protest against the giving of tithes at all, and more especially tithe of moneys received on pawned effects. And very soon she had floundered into a slough of argument that led no way at all.

Egholm strode fuming up and down the room.

"You didn't put it in at all."

"I did. To the last *øre*."

Now this was perfectly true. The money *had* been put in....

"Then you must have stolen it again after."

"God wouldn't have it, I know. It's blood money."

"Wouldn't He? He shall—I'll see that He does! You've stolen money from the Lord! What have you done with it?"

"What do you think we should do with it?"

"Who's been out buying things?" he thundered, turning to the children.

"It wasn't me—not quite," said Sivert, with one thumb deep in his mouth.

"That means it was you, you little whelp. What did you buy with the money?"

"I didn't buy two eggs." Sivert was steadfastly pleading not guilty.

Egholm called to mind that he had had an egg with his dinner. The depth of villainy was clear and plain.

Fru Egholm could hold out no longer. "I—I thought you needed something strengthening, Egholm; you've been looking so poorly. And I took out the thirty øre again and bought two eggs. One you had, and one I gave the children. They need it, too, poor dears."

Egholm felt his brain seething; he gripped his head with both hands, as if fearing it might burst. Every nerve seemed to shudder as at the touch of glowing iron.

"*Ye are cursed with a curse*," he said in a hollow voice.

"Egholm, do be calm...." But his wife's well-meaning effort only made him the more furious. He picked up his stick and struck the table with a crash.

"You should be struck down and smitten to earth—you have brought a curse upon my house!"

"Egholm, do be careful. It's not for my own sake I say it, but remember the state I'm in...."

"What have I to do with the state you're in?" he thundered inconsequently, but laid down his stick. "Out with the money this minute! Do you hear? The money, the money you took!"

"But you know yourself we used all we had for the rent, or I wouldn't have touched the other. I can't dig up money out of the ground."

"Then give me the silver spoon."

This was a little child's spoon, worn thin, and bearing the date of Fru Egholm's christening.

"Take it, then," she said, weeping.

The children had been looking on with frightened eyes. Sivert, in his confusion, now began sawing again.

"What—you dare—at such a time! Stop that at once!" cried his father. And by way of securing immediate obedience, he twined his fingers in the boy's hair and dragged him backwards out of his chair, till his wooden shoes rattled against the flap of the table.

Fru Egholm sprang towards them; the linen she was at work on tore with a scream.

"For Heaven's sake!" she cried desperately, picking up the boy in her arms.

"Give me the spoon and let's have no more nonsense," said Egholm, and strode out. The three stood listening, as to the echoes of retreating thunder. First the slam of the door below, then the heavier clang of the gate across the yard.

"O—oh!" said Hedvig, "he ought to be *thrashed*!" And she drew a deep breath, as of cleaner air.

"Don't speak like that, child. After all, he's your father."

II

Egholm descended the stairs, each step carrying him so much farther down from the heights of his rage. By the time he had crossed the stone paving, and let the street door clang behind him, he was as gentle as any hermit of the dale.

A gust of wind sent him staggering over to the outflow of a gutter pipe, which greeted him with an icy shower; he took it as one might take the jest of a friend. What matter, either, that the same wind thrust a chilly feeler in under his collar, right down to the armhole, or slapped him flat-handed on the mouth and left him breathless? He was not moved to anger when the streams and puddles he was wading through followed the law of nature and filled his leaky boots within to the level of the waters without. Meekly he pressed his hat more firmly down, bowed his head submissively, and walked in all humility close to the house walls, lest he should hinder the wind in its task.

The tumult within him had subsided, leaving no more than the ordinary eagerness of a man in a hurry—a man intent on getting to a meeting in good time.

Street after street, with the same wet breath in his face. He crossed over Vestergade, where the shop windows flared in a row on either side, and a carriage on its way to the theatre nearly knocked him down. Then he burrowed once more into the side streets, emerging at last, by way of a narrow passage, into a yard, where lights were burning in the windows of a stable—a stable converted, being now the hall and meeting-place of the Brethren of St. John.

The unlighted entry gave out a thick smell of mildew and plaster. Egholm felt a childish nervousness as he realised that the meeting had already begun. He smoothed his wreath of hair, and wiped the water from his face with his cape; then, fumbling for the handle of the door, he walked in.

The hall was half-full of people; young Karlsen was standing on the stage, delivering a sort of homily. This was young Karlsen's usual opening, designed to pass the time until old Karlsen could get away from the shop. Everybody knew it, and all bore it patiently, excepting young Karlsen himself, who longed most earnestly for the hour of his deliverance.

At the sound of the door, he stooped and bent forward, trying to see beneath the lamps and make out who had come in. But he made no pause in his sermon; only, his delivery became somewhat strained and disconnected.

When the bald top of Egholm's head caught the light, however, he drew back with a jerk of disappointment, yawned, thrust his hands resignedly into his pockets, and went on:

"Consequently, my dear friends, as I have said——"

Egholm stepped softly to a rickety seat, and sheltered himself behind Fru Laursen's ample figure.

The hall was not large, but all were heartily welcome there. On Saturdays and Sundays its rotten floor-boards shook beneath the feet of factory girls, with high wooden heels, and lads from the slaughterhouse, with neckties slipping up at the back. Both parties sweated profusely as they danced, and mine host from the dramshop across the courtyard sat on an upturned box next the door uncorking bottled beer.

On Wednesdays, from six to eight, a drill sergeant fumed over a class of unpromising pupils from the Peasant Welfare Schools, who walked, and on the toes rose, and from the hips bent, as they were told, yet never managing to attain that explosive *élan* which alone maketh the heart of a drill sergeant to rejoice.

When the Brethren of St. John arrived at eight, the air would be foggy with chalk precipitated in the sweat of peasant brows; it might even happen that the "last four" were still gaspingly at work dragging the vaulting-horse back into place.

For three hours, no more, the congregation of Brethren held the hall in peace; a few minutes past eleven, and figures uncouthly garbed thrust pale but insistent faces in at the door. These were the Histrionics—the Amateur Dramatic Society of the Trade and Commercial Assistants' Union, who with true business talent had chosen Wednesday for their rehearsals, in order to enjoy the warmth provided beforehand by the Brethren. They were not interested in other of the Brethren's manifestations. Any extension of the service or proceedings beyond time limit would be greeted with whistlings, cat-calls, and slamming of doors—while nothing could exceed the eager politeness with which the waiting Histrionics made way for the Brethren as they left.

The hall was further used as an auction room. Egholm was often present on such occasions; he had an inclination towards the feverish excitement of the hammer.

Karlsen was still on his feet.

Egholm let his glance wander absently from the ropes and trapeze to the ragged fringe of the stage curtain, that waved in the draught like the fin of a fish.

He was not an attentive listener; he freely admitted that, when he came to the meetings, it was not so much to hear the edifying speeches of the "Evangelist," as because the door to the treasury of the Lord was here to be found. And the depth of faith in his heart—that was the key.... With a sudden impulse, he felt in his pocket for the tithe-money. Yes, thank Heaven, it was there.

Karlsen was taking an unpardonable time about it this evening. There was an ever-recurring phrase he used: *"Dear friends."* He used it like the knots in the climbing-rope that hung from the ceiling, as something to rest on by the way. And there was often quite an appreciable pause before he could spit on his hands and go on. It was plain to see that his speech would never carry him beyond the roof, but, for all that, his face, bluely unshaven, and furrowed with intercrossing wrinkles, showed a degree of cunning as if he were solving a difficult problem, or recounting the details of a complicated business manœuvre.

Egholm knew that Karlsen had been a travelling pedlar selling woollen goods from his pack along the roads, before he turned Evangelist. And in some ways, the tricks of his old trade clung to him yet. He would hand out eternal truths as if it were a pair of flannel unmentionables—pure wool, unshrinkable, everlasting wear....

Having nothing now with which to occupy his hands, the Evangelist thrust them in his pockets and gesticulated with them under cover there. Now he would clench his fist, till the pocket bulged as if with a heavy revolver; now he would draw out his breeches sideways like a concertina. And in the pauses he could be seen to scratch himself assiduously, first with one hand, then with the other.

At last—at last he came to an end, and led the singing from a little thin book.

The congregation livened up a little, with a clearing of throats and shifting in seats. Half-way through the hymn, the door was heard. The Evangelist ducked down again to look, and when suddenly he pulled his hands out of his pockets, all knew who it was that had arrived.

Old Karlsen, the Evangelist's father, was the eldest of the flock, and holder of its highest dignity—that of Angel.

Also, apart from his connection with the Brethren, proprietor of a very paying little ironmongery business.

Slowly he strode through the hall; the singing faces turned towards him as he came. His black clothes gave him an air of distinction; his silvery hair and prophet's beard were outward and visible signs of holiness. It would be hard to imagine a figure more suited in its dignity to the weighty name of Angel.

The only access to the stage was by way of three beer cases set stairwise to its edge. But under the footsteps of the prophet they were transformed to golden steps of a ladder leading heavenward.

Young Karlsen murmured a few words, glanced at his watch, and disappeared like one cast forth as unworthy. And old Karlsen prayed with his earnest, almost tearful voice for the welfare of the congregation.

Egholm was thrilled. This—this was surely communion with the Lord.

The eyes of the prophet shone in the glare from the footlights—or perhaps it was rather that he saw God, as it had been promised to the pure in heart.

There came a sound of weeping from behind; Egholm turned to see. It was Lystrup, the cobbler. His flat, brown fingers clutched and curled convulsively, and his bony head, with the queer feathery hair, rocked to and fro, as he wept and moaned, without covering his face.

The cobbler's emotion spread to those around. Within a second it had reached the hindmost bench, where the old women from the almshouses sat. There was a flutter of movement among the shawls, accompanied by a low wailing. Egholm noticed with some surprise that deaf old Maren was weeping with the best. Evidently, the influence of Angel Karlsen could manifest itself in other ways than that of common speech.

Egholm was greatly moved; he withdrew his gaze, and looked down at the floor as if in search of something fixed and immovable. But Fru Laursen's back began to work, and soon her bulky frame was slopping incontinently about in front of him. Egholm felt an ache within him, something comparable to hunger; he raised his eyes and seemed to see, through tears, great folded angel-wings behind Karlsen's back. This was too much; Egholm surrendered himself utterly, and wept. And his weeping was louder and more passionate than the weeping of those about him; some there were who ceased at the sound, and watched him.

Young Karlsen had planted himself against the wall by the end of Egholm's bench, and was enjoying the effect. The wrinkles in the young apostle's face were ceaselessly at play, forming new and intricate labyrinths without end. As soon as the Angel had finished his prayer, young Karlsen slipped in close to Egholm and sat down beside him.

"Straight to the heart," he said admiringly. "That's the sort of goods, what? It fetches them."

Egholm dried his eyes bashfully.

"That's the way to drive a lot like this. But"—a sudden gleam of contempt shone in his blue-and-watery sheep's eyes—"it's about the only thing he can do. Angel, indeed! Once he's got you here, he's good for something, I'll allow. But who is it fills the hall?—eh, young man? Who is it gets them here to start with? Jutland and the half of Fyn, that's my district. I'm an Evangelist—a fisher of men. And I've my little gift of tongues as well—and need it, or the fishes wouldn't bite as they do.

"Hear my little speech this evening? Not much in it to speak of. But then I'd finished really, by the time you came. But I've got another on hand that'll do the trick. The Word, what?"

"Yes," sighed Egholm accommodatingly.

"Well, you know yourself," said the Evangelist, with a little laugh, "for you were simply done for when I began. You can't deny it!"

"God's own words——" began Egholm.

"Of course, my dear good man, of course. But who picked them out? God's words, you say, but there's any amount of words; no end of words. The thing is to pick out the right ones—just as you'd pick out the right sort of bait for the right sort of fish. God's words—huh! The Bible's like a pack of cards; doesn't mean anything till it's been dealt round."

Egholm spoke up at this. "I wouldn't like, myself," he said, "to compare the Bible to a pack of cards. But—as far as I know—I'd say there's no card to beat the ace of clubs."

The Evangelist laughed heartily. "If spades are trumps, a bit of a smudgy black knave's enough to do for your ace of clubs. There's one coming along this evening—I've been working on her for over two years now, and all she cared for was the fear of Hell. You've got to deal with them according to their lights, and there's a power of difference sometimes. Now, you, for instance—you were easy enough. Windows of heaven opening, that was your line. Ho, I remember! Well, well, it's all the same, as long as...."

Karlsen broke off in distraction every time the door opened.

"As long as the Lord gets your souls. And Father, he'll see to that."

Egholm began to feel uncomfortable.

The congregation had broken up into groups, centring more particularly about the neighbourhood of the Angel. Johannes, the postman, glared furiously, with distended greenish eyes, at Fru Laursen wading like a cow among the reeds.

"If I can keep behind her," thought Egholm to himself as he rose, "I might get through. Just to thank him...."

"Thought it was her," whispered Karlsen in his ear.

"Eh?"

With a look of unspeakable cunning, Karlsen brought his face closer, blinked his eyes, and whispered again:

"A goldfish! And, on my word, the best we've had up to now. The one I told you about before."

Egholm forgot all else. "A lady, you mean? Who? Coming to-night?"

"A lady, yes," said Karlsen, almost stifling with pride. "A real lady, and no fudge." He made a gesture that might have been mere helplessness. "But whether she'll come or not, well, time will show."

A little after, he lapsed into his natural dialect, and said frankly:

"I'm simply bursting to see if she'll come."

"But who is it?" asked Egholm impatiently.

"Her name—is—Fru Westergaard!"

"What? You don't mean—the Distillery?"

"Hundred thousand," said Karlsen, patting an imaginary pocket-book. "Widow of the late Distiller Westergaard, yes!" Then suddenly he broke into his platform tone, an imitation of Angel Karlsen's tear-stifled voice.

"Fru Westergaard's soul was hungered and athirst after Zion. And for two years past I've cried aloud to her in the wilderness, making ready the way before her—the way to the blessed Brotherhood of St. John. And now, at last, my words have brought forth fruit in her heart. Yes, and *I've been to the villa!*"

He grasped Egholm's hand and pressed it in a long, firm grip—a way they had among the Brethren.

Again the door opened, but it was only Meilby, the photographer. The Evangelist turned up his nose in scorn, and looked another way.

Meilby was another uncommon figure in his way. Here, among a congregation of contritely stooping sinners, he walked as stiffly upright as a well-drilled recruit. Even his eyes had nothing of that humility which might be expected in the house of the Lord, but looked about him sharply, as if in challenge, though ordinarily they were mildly blue as a boy's. What did he want here, night after night? Was he drawn by some higher power, and yet sought, like Saulus, to kick against the pricks? Maybe. Egholm looked after him with a shake of the head, as he tramped through the hall, shut his cigar-case with a click, and seated himself irreverently on the vaulting-horse.

Egholm often walked home with Meilby after the meetings, but it was he who did the talking, Meilby's contributions rarely amounting to more than a fretful "Heh," "Haw," or "Ho"—a kind of barking, incomprehensible to ordinary mortals.

"D'you know Meilby at all?" asked Egholm.

Karlsen twirled one finger circlewise in front of his forehead, but he had not time to explain himself further; just at that moment Fru Westergaard arrived.

She stopped just inside the door, and turned her wet veil up over her eiderdown toque—a tall, thin woman, with the angular movements of an old maid, and clothes that looked as if she slept in them.

"Naughty, naughty dog! Outside, Mirre, Mirre, do you hear!"

She faced round, and waved her dripping umbrella at an eager poodle with its tongue hanging out.

"Here she is!" cried young Karlsen. And at once the room was so still that the scraping of the dog could be heard against the flooring. All mouths stood open, as if in one long indrawn breath of astonishment.

Still scolding under her breath, she walked with some embarrassment a few steps forward. Young Karlsen thrust Egholm aside, and hurried to meet her with a bow.

"Dog's all right," he said, with reassuring ease of manner. "Don't bother about him. Late? Not a bit of it; we've hardly begun. Just sitting talking, heart to heart, you understand. Come along in, both of you. Know me, doggy, don't you, eh?"

He bent down and ruffled the dog's ears.

"He—he must have slipped out and followed me. I'd no idea...."

Young Karlsen's eyeballs rolled about, to see what impression the lady made upon the congregation. And he was not disappointed. If St. John the Apostle, the traditional founder of the sect, had appeared in their midst, it could hardly have created a greater sensation.

Egholm had himself been something of a thunderbolt—an ex-official of the railway service suddenly appearing in this assembly of hunchbacked tailors and lame shoemakers, relics from the almshouses, and all that was worn out and faded—always excepting, of course, the prosperous ironmonger at their head. But Fru Westergaard was as an earthquake that sent them flat on their faces at once. Not a child in the town but knew her and her villa and her dog, that took its meals with her at table.

Johannes, the postman, stood leaning against the wall, helpless, as if in terror.

Madam[1] Kvist, her eyes starting out behind her glasses, asked aloud, in unaffected wonder:

"Why—what in the name of mercy will she be wanting here?"

And Madam Strand, the dustman's wife, a little black figure of a woman, was curtseying and mumbling continually: "Such an honour, did you ever, such an honour...."

Most of those present inwardly endorsed the sentiment.

Egholm drew himself up and sought to catch Fru Westergaard's eye. He did not manage it, but let off his bow all the same. Only the incorrigible photographer sat swinging his legs on the vaulting-horse, with an expression of cold disapproval on his face.

Angel Karlsen stood by the three steps, ready, like another St. Peter, to receive the approaching soul. He took both the lady's hands and pressed them warmly.

"There's rejoicing here on earth and in the mansions of the Lord," he said, with emotion, "at the coming of this our new disciple." When he spoke, his great white beard went up and down, as if emphasising his words.

"And now the usual word of thanksgiving. Sit down here in front, *Frue*."

The new disciple was still talking nervously about the dog—it was leaving footmarks all over the place, but then, you know, in such weather.... She had galoshes for it, really, only to-night....

She moved to sit down, but the others rose hurriedly as she did so, and the bench rocked.

No, no, she couldn't sit there—no, not there; she couldn't. No....

Fru Westergaard allowed herself the luxury of some eccentricities. She had remained unmarried until her six-and-fortieth year.

Egholm had been prepared for the trouble about the seat. Sprightly as a youth, he dashed out of the hall and across the courtyard to the taproom in front.

"A chair; lend me a chair, will you? Fru Westergaard's there."

"Fru Westergaard!"

"Fru Westergaard!"

He came back, breathless, with an American rocking-chair, which he proffered humbly.

The congregation had meanwhile arranged itself in a phalanx formation like wild geese on the wing. In the forefront of all sat the new disciple in her restless chair. On the next bench were Evangelist Karlsen and Egholm alone, and behind them again came the rest of the dearly beloved, in order of precedence according to dignity or ambition.

The entire flock seemed shaping its course towards the sun, in the person of Angel Karlsen, who was up on the platform praying and preaching, tearful and affecting as ever.

"*As the hart panteth after the water brooks, so panteth my soul after Thee, O God.*

"*My soul thirsteth for God, for the living God; when shall I come and appear before God?*"

He wrung his hands in a great agony, and hid his face.

"*My tears have been my meat day and night....*"

Egholm was touched. He, too, knew what it was to weep for meat.

Karlsen the Elder closed with the Lord's Prayer; and another hymn was sung.

"Now, it's me again," whispered the young Evangelist. "You see me let her have it this time."

His speech seemed actually to have gained force and balance; there was an evident purpose in it. The opening was weak, perhaps, for here he still clung to his "Dear friends" from force of habit, though every word was addressed to Fru Westergaard only.

"And now, in conclusion, I thank you, my dear friends, for coming here among us the first time. I hope, dear friends, it may not be the last. In the midst of all your wealth and luxury and manifold delights out at the villa, you have yet felt the lack of a word—the word of the Spirit. Yes, dear friends, it is even so. You go to church and you go back home again, and your need is not fulfilled.

"But then one day there comes to your door—out at the villa—a poor Evangelist, an unlearned man. And lo—a strange thing, dear friends—*he* has the word—the word of the Spirit!"

Having thus laid down a flattering position for himself, young Karlsen went on to praise his new convert as one docile and of a good heart. She had come this evening of all evenings—a first Wednesday—on purpose that she might pay her tithe. No, there was no drawing back. And in truth it would be a fool's game to try it on. The Lord, He could see straight through a drawer in a table or the cover of a bank-book, never fear of that. And what was His, that He was going to have. Yes, that was His way. And woe unto him that falleth into the hands of the living God!

Far down by the door, old Karlsen was modestly seated on the extreme end of a bench. In his lap was a japanned tin box. There was a slight rattle during the next hymn, as he took out his keys and opened the casket.

The bench was so placed that the disciples could only pass by in single file. The old women from the almshouses, who had been sitting farthest back, were now the first to pass. As a matter of fact, they were exempt from the tithe contribution, having no income beyond their food and lodging. But most of them, nevertheless, managed to deposit a copper two or five *øre* piece with the Angel as they went out, though he never so much as looked up.

Why should he look? The money was not for himself, but for God. He was only sitting there holding the black tin box.

There was a clicking of purse-clips, and a soft ring of coin. Lystrup, the cobbler, dropped his money, and crawled miserably over the floor beneath the benches, looking for that which was lost.

Those who had paid stopped behind to see the others share their fate.

Fru Westergaard, Egholm, and the Evangelist came down together.

"But—but how do you manage when it doesn't work out exactly?" said the lady, nervously trying to do sums in her head.

"It always works out exactly," said Karlsen, with superior calm.

"As long as it's *kroner*, of course, I understand. But when it's *kroner and øre*?"

She gave it up as hopeless, and drew out a crumpled book from the little bag she carried.

"Here you are; you can see. I get my money from the bank, you know; it's in a book like this."

Egholm craned up on tiptoe. The Evangelist wormed up closer, his face a curious mingling of venom and sweetness; even old Karlsen thrust the box under his arm and rose to his feet.

"My spectacles!" And he slapped his pockets so that the money rattled in the box.

Two hundred and sixty-six *kroner* thirty *øre*.

That was the figure that showed again and again down the page in the cross-shaded columns, with Fru Westergaard's signature after. There was a murmur from the waiting crowd.

"How much was it?"

"Eh, to think now! And every month!"

"Over two hundred and fifty, that is," explained Lystrup, the cobbler.

"That will be twenty-six *kroner* sixty-three to us," said the Evangelist, as if it were the merest trifle.

"Not sixty-three *øre*?—that can't be," said the disciple energetically, looking round for support.

Egholm could not meet her eyes; it pained him that Karlsen was so evidently right.

"But I only get thirty *øre*, and you say I'm to pay out sixty-three! No, thank you, that's trying it on, I know."

"It's the law—it's the law." Old Karlsen drummed on his box.

"Oh, I won't put up with it!" Fru Westergaard's grey cheeks flushed with a red spot.

"Not an *øre* less."

Young Karlsen stood planted in the opening between the bench and the wall. He wore high boots, with his trousers thrust into them, and stood with his feet a little apart. There was something ominous written, as it were, between the lines in his face. His shoulders were slightly raised—a very respectable pair of shoulders had young Karlsen.

Fru Westergaard tucked away her book again with trembling hands.

"Perhaps you'll let me pass?"

"It's twenty-six sixty-three, all the same," said the Evangelist, without moving an inch.

"I won't give more than twenty-six thirty!" She stamped her foot. Mirre growled softly, and sniffed round and round Karlsen's legs.

"Twenty-six sixty-three."

"Sh!" old Karlsen intervened. "We'll take what *Fruen* thinks is right. The Lord is long-suffering.... Lauritz, you can be putting out the corner lights."

Thus did the Angel, by his wisdom and gentleness, save one soul for the congregation of the Brethren.

Fru Westergaard had, it appeared, the money in a separate compartment of her bag, all ready counted out. Handing them to Angel Karlsen, she said:

"And you're quite sure there's no Hell, really?"

"No Hell...."

Young Karlsen was standing on a bench, puffing at one of the lights. He turned warningly towards his father.

"No," he cried. "That's right. No Hell. You know, we talked it over...."

Angel Karlsen bowed his head in silence, but Fru Westergaard stared wildly before her.

"Hell, hell fire, all yellow flames...."

Egholm could contain himself no longer. He would show the lady and the rest of them how a true disciple settled up his accounts with God. With a smile and a gesture as if he had been casting a rose into his mistress' lap, he flung his paper bag of money into the Angel's casket. The bag burst with the shock, and the coins came twirling out; the old man had to use both hands to guard them, and could hardly close the box.

"Wait, there's more yet!" cried Egholm, and his voice broke. He held the silver spoon aloft in two fingers, then pressed it in through the crack at the lid of the box.

But the box was full to repletion, and the bowl of the spoon would not go in.

Egholm felt there had never been so magnificent an offering.

Yet another of the Brethren passed by that strait place—Meilby, the photographer. Not one single copper *øre* did he put in, but Angel Karlsen only turned his eyes meekly to the other side.

III

February had set in. Fru Egholm's seventh was making ever stronger demands on her heart's blood. While she toiled at her work, the young citizen to come was pleased to kick about occasionally, or turn over on the other side, making her faint and dizzy. But, recovering, she would smile, and whisper softly: "There there, now, bide your time, little man." She had her own convictions that it was to be a boy.

Egholm stood in front of the mirror, smoothing his wreath of hair. His pupil was due for the English lesson.

"The Pupil" was a subject of considerable importance in the house, especially to Egholm's own mind. It was no other than Meilby, the sharp-tongued photographer, who had started taking lessons in the previous November. After many mysterious hints, and exacting a promise of silence, he had confided to Egholm that he was going to America in a few months' time. Egholm had grabbed at him avidly and without ceremony, as a chance of work. Regarded as a pupil, he was by no means promising. He had but the faintest conception of any difference between parts of speech such as substantives and adjectives, and whenever his mentor touched on genitives and possessives, he would glance absently towards the door. Furthermore, he never paid any fees, which was a subject of constant tribulation between Anna and her husband.

"But it's a good thing to have a little outstanding. Like capital in the bank, against a rainy day."

Anna made no answer to this. It seemed to her mind that the days were rainy enough to call for all the capital by any means available.

Egholm sniffed vigorously, and postponed the matter further. But now it was February, and he must raise the question somehow. He smoothed his hair with extra attention, to make the most of his dignity when the pupil arrived. Unfortunately, he could hardly point to the goods delivered and demand payment in cash—the goods were so little in evidence.

It passed off better than he had expected. Meilby said "Good evening" in English when he arrived, and laughed a little nervously, as if dismayed at his own courage. Egholm snatched at the opening, and came to the point at once:

"That's right, that's right—you're getting on. Getting on, yes. But don't you think, now, you might let me have a little on account?"

Meilby laughed no more. Money—it was always such a nuisance about money. There didn't seem to be any money these days. Money was a thing extinct, he said.

"On earth, yes," Egholm admitted.

But no need to bother about that. It would be all right. Only wait to the end of the month, and then it would be decided. "Whether I'm to go or not," said Meilby.

Of course, he didn't want to go. Much rather stay where he was. But, of course, he would go all the same. What else could he do? And if he went, why, then, of course, Egholm would get his money. That was how it stood. How else could it be?

Egholm was very far from understanding, but he gave it up. Opening the book, he got to work at the lesson, but with less careful attention, perhaps, than usual. And after a little he broke in, cutting short his pupil in the middle of a sentence:

"But about the money—how will you get the money if you do go?"

"Why, then, of course, I shall sell all my apparatus."

So that was it. Egholm still seemed troubled in his mind. He knew the collection of things that formed Meilby's stock-in-trade. There was one item in particular—that devilish camera of his. It was quite a small one, but with a breadth of focus that could almost look round a corner. Fancy having that for his own! There would be an end of poverty then!

The windows of heaven should be opened, and the flood pour in—oh, in no time. He knew it, he felt sure of it. But the belly was not to be put off, not for so much as a day. And his hands were impatient too; there was a nervous thrill at the roots of the nails, or a deadly chill in the fingers from sheer inactivity. Every morning he raced about after the situations vacant in the papers, but always in vain. With Meilby's apparatus, he could make money—ay, though his studio had no roof but the February sky.

He grew quite genial towards his pupil, and praised him more than was properly his due. When they had finished with their brainwork for the evening, he said anxiously:

"But, promise me you don't go selling them without letting me know."

Meilby would bear it in mind.

"Yes, but suppose you forgot?"

"Why, we'll be none the less friends for that," said Meilby, with an amiable smile.

"You'll get nothing out of him, you see," said Anna when he had gone. "It'll be just the same with him as with young Karlsen, when he came to learn English, too. Huh! It was you that learned something that time, if you ask me."

"He's an artful one," said Egholm, with a laugh. "He tricked the doctor when he went to be examined. But, after all—what's a trifle like that when a man stands firm on the rock of truth?"

"Do you think Meilby does? You think it's for any good he's going running off to America like that?"

Egholm, law-abiding man, paled at the thought, but said, with an attempt at liveliness:

"I'll get him to stay, then."

"But he won't pay you at all unless he goes."

That, again, was true—painfully true. No ... anyhow, Egholm would have nothing to do with any doubtful affairs. Not for any price. Better let Meilby go his own gait as soon as he pleased.

But even as he formed the thought, he seemed to feel the milled edges of the screws that set the camera between his fingers, and with a sigh he breathed the resolution from him once more.

One morning, a few days later, Egholm came back from his usual round.

"No luck, I suppose?"

"No, no, no," he snarled, flinging off his hat. Then he took down the Bible.

What could have happened to make his hands shake like that?

A few minutes later came the explanation.

"I went after a job—Hansen and Tvede, it was—as errand boy. Told them they could have me a full day's work just for my food. But they laughed at me. Oh, and there was a beast of a fellow in riding-boots—the manager, perhaps. You should have seen his face."

"Perhaps he meant it wasn't the sort of thing they could offer you. Something better," hinted Fru Egholm.

He made no answer, but strove to calm his indignation by strenuous attention to the Bible. If that didn't help him, why, then.... But he was nearly through with it now—it was the Epistle to the Hebrews.

The letters danced and crept like ants before his eyes.

"*And verily they that are of the sons of Levi, who receive the office of the priesthood, have a commandment to take tithes of the people according to the law, that is, of their brethren....*"

"Ha ha! Riding-boots and all! No, 'twasn't that he meant, giving me something better. The beast! I shan't forget him!"

"*For the priesthood being changed, there is made of necessity a change also of the law....*"

"'I see from the paper you're wanting an errand boy'—that's what I said to him. And asked if I would do. And I crushed my hat in my hands and stood up. Then, of course, what he ought to have said was, 'What, *you* looking for a place as errand boy? No, no. Couldn't think of it. I'll take you on in the office, as a clerk. You shall be cashier. I've taken a fancy to you, the way you stand there modestly as could be.' But he didn't say that, not a word of it. Good Lord, no! The worst of it was, he saw through me. *He winked at me!*"

"*For there is verily a disannulling of the commandment going before for the weakness and unprofitableness thereof.*

"*For the law made nothing perfect, but the bringing in of a better hope did; by the which we draw nigh unto God.*"

Egholm sighed, and passed his hand over his face. Alas, he noted to his shame how his thoughts had strayed from the Bible's lofty theme.

What could it be for a commandment, that was disannulled for the weakness and unprofitableness thereof, he wondered. H'm, it would say farther on, no doubt. And he read on, but it did not appear to say. Then he went back and began again, reading slowly, in a whisper, the same verses over again. And of a sudden, his heart contracted violently, forcing a spout of blood to his temples. What—what was this? Was it *the tithe* that was abolished?

He read it through again and again.

"Anna"—he dared not trust his own senses now—"Anna, come here and look at this. Quick—read from there to there." He stood as if about to strike; there were red spots on his pale face. Anna trembled with fear, and fell to reading about Melchisedec, the Levites, and the rest, without understanding a word of it all.

"Well, why don't you speak, woman?" broke in Egholm, when she had been reading a few seconds. "Are you asleep?—or, perhaps it doesn't interest you? Eh? Now, then, what is it you're reading?—what do you make of it? Eh?"

"Yes, yes, I see," stammered Fru Egholm, her eyes flitting to another part altogether in her confusion—"something about the Tabernacle...."

"Is the tithe abolished?—that's what I want to know," said Egholm insistently. "Does it say there, or does it not, that the tithe is weak and unprofitable?"

"Why, yes—but that's what I've always said," answered she, with marvellous presence of mind. "Was it only that you wanted me to see?"

Egholm looked her up and down contemptuously.

A moment later he was tearing down the street with the big family Bible all uncovered under one arm.

Oh, but this was the most wonderful day of his life! The Bible itself had revealed its darkest secrets to him—*to him alone*. What would they say, all those whose minds were yet in darkness? what would old Angel Karlsen say? what would young Evangelist Karlsen look like with his wrinkled face—

when they heard that the Community of the Brethren of St. John was built on sand—nay, upon a swamp, into the bottomless depth of which their money sank never to be seen again? *He, Egholm, was a new Luther*, wielding the Bible as a mighty club against heresy and false doctrine. They would have to make him Angel, ay, Archangel, after this. In every land where the Brethren of St. John were known, his name would be named with honour. He would write a new Book of Laws for the Brotherhood, and it should be translated into seven tongues. Into seven tongues! Almost like a new Bible.

Karlsen's shop was at a corner of the market square. It was a very old house, with a steep red roof. At the bottom two small windows had been let in to make it look like a shop, and through them one could discern, in spite of a thick layer of cobwebs and dust, the rows of shelves with yellow jars in all sizes. The modest store was suited to the taste of the peasant customers. They could stand for ages pondering over the choice of a shovel or rake, and weighing it in the hand. Karlsen was understood to be a wealthy man.

Egholm inquired of a chilblainy youth if he could speak with Angel Karlsen.

H'm. He didn't know. Would go in and ask.

"Say it's something of importance," said Egholm.

As the door in the corner was opened, Egholm heard a sound of voices in dispute from the office beyond. Two voices—and he could not recognise either. Or was it—yes, surely that was old Karlsen's, after all? Egholm listened in wonder, as one might listen to a familiar air played out of time or at a different pace.

"Call me a scoundrel if you like," shouted the one, a nasal trumpeting voice with a twang of city jargon—"call me a thief, a convict, or anything you damn well please, but I won't be called a fool!"

"But the contract, the contract, the contract!" screamed out the angelic voice of Karlsen the Elder.

No, the young man was sorry, Hr. Karlsen could not possibly see him just now. He was engaged with one of the travellers.

"Well, I must see him, anyhow," said Egholm more soberly.

They were at it again inside, and his knock was unheeded. Then suddenly the whole seemed to collapse in a cascade of laughter.

He knocked again, and walked in. There was old Karlsen, his face unevenly flushed, with a fat cigar sticking out of his beard, and before him a bright-eyed, elegantly dressed commercial traveller, who slapped the Angel's outstretched hand repeatedly, both men laughing at the top of their voices.

"Beg pardon, Hr. Karlsen—er—would you kindly read this?..." Where was it now? Egholm began helplessly turning the pages of his Bible.

"Hullo, here's somebody wants to save our souls, by the look of it," said the elegant one, with a tentative laugh.

"Didn't my young man out there tell you I was engaged?" said old Karlsen angrily, turning aside.

"But it's a discovery I've made—it's of the utmost importance. A wonderful find—here in the Holy Scripture itself. Read it, here—it's only a few lines. I can hardly believe my own senses. Read it—there!"

"But, my dear friend," said the Angel, "you can see for yourself I'm engaged. We're in the middle of important business."

"Let me read just three words to you."

"No, no, no, I won't have it, I say."

Egholm stood with hectic cheeks; his former respect for the Angel still checked any actual outburst of fury, but from the look of him, it was doubtful what might happen next.

"This is not the proper place to discuss the word of God, nor the proper time, nor the mood for it, either. Come round again this evening, my dear Egholm. At eight, say, and then we can talk over whatever it is that's troubling you."

The commercial plucked him by the sleeve. "I thought you were coming round to the hotel—*Postgaarden*, you said."

"Er—well, we might say *to-morrow* evening at eight," corrected the Angel. "Yes, come round to-morrow, Egholm; that will do."

Egholm drew himself up and shot sparks, but said nothing. He shut up the clasp of his Bible with a snap.

"Have a cigar, won't you?" said the Angel, offering the box.

"No, thank you."

"Yes, yes, do. They're none so bad—what, Hr. Nathan?"

Hr. Nathan uttered a curious sound—an articulate shudder, as it were—and looked quizzically at the box.

"I don't smoke."

"Well, then, a glass of port?"

"I've other things to think about than drinking wine. The fate of the Brotherhood lies in my hand. In *my* hand. I'm going round to the Deacon now."

"No, really? He he! Are you really? Well, well," said Karlsen, with that strangely jovial angel voice of his, that Egholm knew so well, and yet found strange....

IV

But Egholm was so shaken by his interview with the Angel that he did not go round to the Deacon after all. The Deacon was a pottery worker, living at a village just outside the town.

He went back home to look again and make sure it was right. He clutched the Bible tightly under his arm as he walked, as if in dread lest the all-important text might drop out.

Yes, there it was. He read through the passage again in wonder, and fell to musing anew.

That same evening Evangelist Karlsen came round.

Egholm shook his head nervously.

"It's no good, Karlsen. No. I'm not going to give in."

Young Karlsen stood staring open mouthed.

"No. I've settled up with myself once and for all. I won't give in. I know well enough what you've come for."

"But, my dear friends, what on earth are you talking about? Anything wrong?"

"Karlsen, you know as well as I do it's your father sent you round," said Egholm almost pleadingly.

"I swear I know nothing of the sort. I've only just got back this evening. From Veile. Know Justesen, the horsedealer, there? Been seeing him. And then on the way—I've been dragging my bag along, and it's heavy. I thought I'd just look in for a breather."

"Let Sivert carry it for you," said Fru Egholm.

"No, thanks, it's all right outside on the stairs. I never like to leave it very long."

Egholm put his hand to his eyes; the cracked and furrowed countenance of the Evangelist always distracted his attention. Then he began telling of his discovery—first, in mysterious roundabout hints, then suddenly breaking out into fiery declamation, with the open book before him, and his finger-nail underlining the words.

Karlsen was thunderstruck. And he thought *he* knew his Bible.... Never in his life had he come across that place. He stamped about the room, spitting into all four corners.

Egholm went further; he drew up an outline of the new laws, the entire reorganisation....

"It'll be a hard struggle for me, I know. But I'll...."

"Oh, we'll manage it all right," said Karlsen cheerfully.

"Eh? D'you mean to say ... you're on my side?"

"Oh, I'm on the side of the Bible, of course."

And there was Egholm with the enemy's leading general won over, without a blow!

"It's the only thing to do, anyway," explained Karlsen, "as things are now. There's been some talk about you having my place when I moved up. But I don't know what they'll say to that now...."

"Me! Evangelist!" Egholm turned stiff all over.

"Yes," said Karlsen quietly.

"I've never heard a word about it before."

"Well, the Elders have gathered together.... But it was to be a surprise, you understand?"

"Yes, yes," murmured Egholm faintly. Again it overwhelmed him for the moment, but he recovered himself, and said, with a laugh:

"Who knows, they might make me Angel now."

"Almost sure to, I should say," opined the dark Evangelist.

Egholm felt calm and strong now, no longer dizzy as he had been during the morning. And Karlsen was really a jolly sort, after all. Here he was, actually gloating over the face his respected father, the Angel, would set up when the bombshell burst.

The upshot of it was that they worked out a plan together.

Egholm was to prepare a grand speech for the meeting next Wednesday. Karlsen knew—now he came to think of it—quite a lot of first-rate texts that could be used, in support of the new discovery.

"But don't you think"—Egholm lowered his voice confidentially —"wouldn't it be better if I went round to the Brethren, and just let them know how it stands?"

Karlsen pondered.

"H'm. I should say, the best way's to take the whole congregation by surprise, all at once. Better effect, you know, when you can stand there and throw out a hand and there it is! And you've quite a decent platform manner, to my mind."

"Yes," agreed Egholm, beaming.

"Anyhow, I'll trot round and tackle a few of the thickest heads myself. I've a certain amount of influence, you know, and authority, and all that. I know how to manage them."

"Why, then, it's as good as done!" Egholm's voice was almost a song.

"Easy as winking," said Karlsen confidently.

"You don't know how glad I am you came over to the right side at once."

"Oh, never mind about that. You can always do me a little service some time in return."

They stayed up till nearly midnight. Egholm strode up and down, filling the room with words. Possibly he was already rehearsing for the coming Wednesday. Karlsen smoked, and drank many cups of black coffee. The children hung over the table, limp and heavy with drowsiness, casting greedy glances at the settee. Their mother tore at her sewing more violently than usual, and sighed aloud.

At last Karlsen took his leave. Egholm could not bear to break off even then, but went out with him. He waved his arms in the air, and tripped about, now and then actually circling round his companion as they walked.

Did he think, now, the Bible Society would care to have a dissertation on the two conflicting points? There ought, at any rate, to be some kind of indication, an asterisk, say, in the first place, to save others from confusion.

Karlsen thought they very likely would.

The street lamps glowed red in the fog. A policeman appeared at a corner, waved to them cheerfully, and said sympathetically: "Get along home; that's the best place for you."

"Thinks we're drunk," said Egholm, and stopped for breath. "But—we've been talking, and never thought … your bag. We've forgotten all about it."

"Bag? Oh yes…. No; that's all right. I spotted the old man's cart just outside the station, and sent it home by that."

"Good! Then that's all right." Egholm's thoughts were at once occupied with something else. His brain was fluttering with innumerable winged thoughts.

"Well, better say good-night."

"Good-night, Karlsen. And thanks, thanks. You shall be Angel, if I can put in a word."

Egholm looked round, confused. Where had they got to now? These big houses ... it wasn't the way....

"I'll see you right home," he offered.

"Well—er—I'm not exactly going home just yet," said the Evangelist, with some embarrassment. "Just a hand at cards with a few friends, that's all." He sighed guiltily. "But if I do win a *kroner*, say, it means ten *øre* to the Brethren.... Oh, I forgot, that's all over now, of course."

"But—d'you mean to say there's anybody up at this time of night?" asked Egholm in astonishment.

"Only a couple of friends—Brethren in the Lord."

"But where?"

"In the red room at the Hotel *Postgaarden*," said Karlsen innocently.

V

Going round to the meeting on the following Wednesday, Egholm was surprised to find the hall already full, though it was not yet eight o'clock. He was also surprised, and agreeably so, to perceive that his entry created some stir. Evidently, Karlsen had let fall a word of what was to happen. Unless, indeed, it were the Lord Himself that had given hint of it to each individually. Anyhow, it was just as well to have plenty of witnesses in a case like this.

But where—where were the Elders of the flock?

Egholm sat down at the back of the hall, by the stove; it was a pious impulse that had come to him, having in mind the promise that whoso humbleth himself shall be exalted. And it was a good idea in other ways, he thought. The little group of paupers would form an excellent background.

"Angel Karlsen—hasn't he come yet?" he whispered to a shawl-wrapped crone at his side.

The woman looked round, showing a face weather-worn and overgrown like a relic of the past. A single tooth showed like a stone wedge in her half-open mouth. She made no answer.

Egholm repeated his question, with no more result than before. Oh, but, of course, it was Deaf Maren. He had forgotten for the moment. But how ugly she looked to-night—and what a malicious glance she gave him. And the others, too, all with the same forbidding look—why couldn't they answer? It was plain to see they had heard his question, and that they knew enough to tell him if they would. But every one of them turned away, or looked down at the floor—until at last Madam Strand, the gipsy woman, who was sitting on a bench at the extreme left, crept up to him with a submissive curtsey.

"They're in there—all of them," she said, with a shake of her thin grey locks. "All the God-fearing lot—the Angel, and the Prophet from Copenhagen—bless 'em—and the Deacon and young Karlsen. Talking and talking and making their plans. Such a fuss they're making to-night—enough to make a body quake all over."

She passed her wrinkled skinny hand over his wrist as she spoke.

Egholm felt his heart beat faster. He glanced over towards the door Madam Strand had indicated; it led to a little anteroom that was used, among other things, as a dressing-room for the gymnasium class. He fancied he could hear voices. A moment ago he had felt something like pity for all these people, whose conviction he would now be called upon to shatter and replace by another. But already he found himself in need of courage, seeking comfort from the fact that, after all, the weapon was in his hand. What did it matter if there were many who came up against him? And young Karlsen, no doubt, would help to bear the brunt of it.

This last was merely a sort of aside to himself. But Egholm felt his doubts of the Evangelist's honesty suddenly grown stronger than ever.

Those artful round eyes of his—and the queer look in them when he had said good-night that evening outside Hotel *Postgaarden*. What could one expect from a man who went off to play cards at twelve o'clock at night at hotels? And what sort of companions could he find for the same? "Brethren in the Lord," indeed! It was an expensive place, too, that one could hardly expect the poorer Brethren to frequent. Wait a bit, though: *Postgaarden* ... wasn't it there the commercial traveller man was going to meet old Karlsen that same evening?... To sum up, then, nothing more nor less than a neat piece of spying, and carrying the whole tale to his father immediately after! After which, of course, he had simply been sent round to all these simple souls, to set their minds against him, Egholm....

It would be a hard fight now.

Fru Westergaard and Mirre, the dog, passed by. Egholm rose and bowed, but received only a half-glance in return. Fru Westergaard made her way through to her privileged chair, and sat down carefully, arranging her skirts about the dog's head.

Her arrival was like that of the bride at a wedding, the signal for proceedings to begin. At the same moment, the door of the little room opened, and a little troop of men—looking, to tell the truth, more like mutes at a funeral than anything to do with weddings—marched in close order up on to the stage. At their head the Angel, wrapped in his beard, which seemed alive with electric tension. After him marched the Prophet from Copenhagen—a quondam priest by the name of Finck—together with the Deacon, Potter Kaasmose, whose long hair was plastered down and cut as if to the rim of one of his own pots. Of the remaining five, Egholm knew only two—Dideriksen, the Apostle, and Karlsen, the Evangelist. Dideriksen was a very pious man, as was apparent, for instance, in his habit of constantly stroking downwards over his face. Karlsen had put on a glaring red tie, which gave him a martial touch. He looked as if he were gloating over some great disaster. The stairs had been widened with a further consignment of beer boxes, so that the procession could mount the platform in something like order.

A breathless silence reigned among the congregation when Angel Karlsen began to pray, while the remaining Elders seated themselves in a half-circle. The Copenhagen Prophet, evidently on easy and familiar terms with platforms, thrust his coat-tails carelessly aside, polished his gold pince-nez with a handkerchief of brilliant whiteness, and did other things hitherto unknown in those surroundings. Young Karlsen, for instance—not to speak of Potter Kaasmose—would have been utterly unable to imitate the elegant movement with which he flung one leg over the other, after first pulling up the legs of his trousers. He had chosen his seat on the extreme right, like the first violin in an orchestra. His interesting appearance could hardly fail to draw off some attention from the prayer, but was no doubt edifying in itself.

"Amen," said Angel Karlsen.

"And having now concluded this prayer which Thou Thyself hast taught us, we further pray that this our ancient congregation, founded by St. John the Apostle, and lasting even unto this day in despite of the deluge of sin and the drought of indifference, may likewise henceforward so prevail against the ravages of the wolf that steals abroad by night, that neither sheep nor lamb may fall a prey.

"All ye who were present here last evening know what I mean. But for those others who do not, I will briefly set forth the matter which has called us Elders to gather in conclave here to-night."

Egholm sat gasping as if half stunned. "Present here *last evening*!..." Then they had called a meeting, without his knowledge—a meeting where they had betrayed him and his great cause, and sowed the seed of hatred against him in all the hearts of those who had no judgment of their own. In the midst of his anger, indignation, and fear, Egholm yet tried to frame a prayer for strength and courage. But he could do no more than mumble helplessly: "I'm in the right, you know I am. Lord God, you know I'm in the right."

Meanwhile, old Karlsen was reciting a pretty parable about the wolf that took upon itself sheep's clothing, that it might deceive the unwary—ay, even the shepherd himself, that he might open the door of the fold and let that monster enter in, with kindly words: "Enter, poor strayed sheep, and be refreshed with the grass of this pleasant fold." But then one day the shepherd looked into the eyes of that wolf in sheep's clothing, and lo! they were eyes of fire. And another day he looked at its teeth, and lo! they were the teeth of a wolf. But the monster believed itself still safe and unsuspected—even until to-night. "And so it comes here amongst us at this moment, and says to the sheep: 'Follow me. I know a place where the grass is richer and more pleasant; make haste and leave that evil shepherd, who shears you of your fleece. I will lead you; I will be your shepherd!'"

When the Angel had finished, Egholm rose, pale and ill at ease, and begged leave to speak. But his seat was so far back, and his voice so weak, that those on the platform might be excused for overlooking him. All heard, however, when young Karlsen called out the number of a hymn, and though Egholm repeated his request in a slightly louder voice, the congregation began singing:

> "'Up, ye Christians, up and doing,
> Warriors of the Lord, to arms!
> Lo, the foeman's host pursuing,
> All the power of war's alarms.
> >   Draw and smite
> >   For the right,
> Hell is arming 'gainst the Light.
>
> Follow in your leader's train,
> Trusting in his strength to win,
> Satan hopes the day to gain,
> Up, and smite the host of sin!
> >   Here at hand
> >   Still doth stand
> One who can all powers command!'"

Egholm had lost patience. As the hymn concluded, he sprang up and roared across the hall:

"Look here, do you mean to say *I'm* Satan?"

There was a stir as all in the hall turned round. Fru Westergaard's chair rocked suddenly, and a bench crashed down, but after that followed a moment of icy silence, cleft immediately by Karlsen's angel trumpet:

"Guilty conscience, Egholm?"

A new silence, Egholm stammering and gurgling, but finding no appropriate answer. Then the Evangelist let loose a shower of insulting laughter. Strangely enough, this had the effect of bringing Egholm to his senses.

"I was the first to ask; it's your place to answer. D'you mean to say I'm Satan?"

And before any of the Elders on the platform could pull themselves sufficiently together, he went on:

"Do you know this book here? It's an old one, and the title-page is missing. You think, perhaps, it's St. Cyprian, but I can tell you, it's the Holy Scripture. Yes, that's what it is. And what I have to say to you now is just the words of the Scriptures, and no more. Holy Scripture, pure and undefiled. I'll read it out, and you can judge for yourselves. I tell you, you haven't got a shepherd at all; you've a *butcher*!"

At the first exchange of words, the congregation had been confused and uneasy, quivering this way and that like a magnetic needle exposed to intermittent current. Now, Egholm had, it is true, most of them facing his way, but many looked up to the Elders, and especially to the Angel, partly to see the effect of Egholm's words, and partly to gain some hint as to which way their own feeling should tend. The congregation was thus divided, but Egholm wanted it united. Accordingly, he left his place between Deaf Maren and the stove, and advanced by jerks, still speaking, up towards his foes.

Yes, he knew it was a serious thing to call Angel Karlsen—Egholm shook a little at the venerable words—a butcher. But it was plain to him now, after what had passed, that Angel Karlsen was not acting in good faith as regards the point in dispute: whether tithe should be paid, or if tithe had been abolished by God's own word, and was consequently foolish—nay, wicked. But if the Angel knew God's will, and did not act upon it, and open the eyes of the Brotherhood to the same, then no words could be too strong.

Egholm spoke for twenty minutes. He had got right to the front, and stepped up on to the first of the beer boxes, making, as it were, an act drop of his body in front of those on the platform. The audience could only see their shadows, and hear a slight sound when the Copenhagen Prophet cleared his throat. Once young Karlsen tried his devilish laugh, but was sternly suppressed by his venerable sire. There was no real disturbance of any sort; the congregation made but one listening, eager face. The Elders were exorcised already. Victory—victory!

But at the very moment when the thought first thrilled him, Egholm's eloquence suddenly ran dry. With a spasm of dread he realised that he could say no more. The source within him, that he had imagined endless, had ceased. He had not firmness enough to begin again, and the texts and parables he had chosen for his purpose had been rehearsed so often in his mind for the occasion that he could not now remember what he had actually said and what he could still use.

The emptiness that followed was almost physically oppressive—Egholm gasped once or twice as if the very air about him were gone. Then came the voice of the Angel, calm and firm:

"Have you any more to say?"

"No," said Egholm, paling as he spoke. "I hope now you have understood."

And with that he stepped down from his elevation, sighed, wiped his forehead nervously, and leaned up against the wall at the side.

Old Karlsen delivered a prayer longer and more powerful than ever before. It gathered like a cloud above the congregation, gradually obscuring all that Egholm had said. Not until he noticed that the cloud had condensed here and there to a mild rain of tears did the Angel pass over imperceptibly to mention of Egholm's onslaught.

"And now, now—well, you have heard the leader of your flock, the shepherd and Angel of the Brotherhood, referred to as a butcher. Here, in our own house, and out of the mouth of one whom we regarded as a brother. Why do I not lift up my hand against him, and drive him forth, even as the Master drove out those from the Temple who defiled its holy places? No! For it is written: *Blessed are the meek*."

The Angel's prayer had opened the hearts of the flock. Thereupon Finck the Prophet stepped forward. He wore a reddish-brown beard, his eyebrows were bushy, and his eyes glittered behind his glasses. It seemed as if he had hitherto affected lordly indifference, but was now so moved that he could no longer control his emotion, and his anger burst forth in a torrent.

"In days gone by," he began, "when I realised that the Established Church of Denmark was being suffered to drift like a ship without a compass, I declined to stay on board. And before leaving, I warned my fellow-travellers, and the captain and the mate. I told them in plain, bold words that they were drifting towards shipwreck. Many believed that my words were over-bold. A conflict raged about my name, as some of you may perhaps remember. But, now, we have heard a man whose words were not bold, but only brutal and coarse—a man who, I think I am qualified to say, lacks the very rudiments of ability to understand what he reads. This ignoramus takes upon himself to pick out a verse here and a verse there, and then adds them together in a fashion of his own. We may compare him with the man who read one day in his Bible: 'Cain rose up against Abel his brother, and slew him'—and the next: 'Go thou and do likewise.'...."

The sum and essence of Finck's oration was that the rendering of tithe was a jewel of price reserved for the Brotherhood of St. John apart from all others. To cast away that jewel now would be sheer madness.

Egholm stood quivering with impatience to answer. His mind was clear now as to what he should say. And as soon as Finck had ended, he sprang forward.

"It seems to me that Hr. Finck, the Prophet, in spite of all his claims to learning, and his libellous attack...."

"Silence, man!" roared Finck, his voice echoing roundly from the walls. "We will hear no more. You have said your last word here. Go!"

"My turn now," said young Karlsen, with a swaggering fling of his shoulders.

But the venerable Angel could not find it in his heart to deny Egholm a last word. He found it preferable to let him wreak his own destruction. And with his keen perception of the feeling among the congregation, he was confident that this would be the result.

"Beloved Brethren," he said, "there is but a quarter of an hour left us—one poor quarter of an hour. I had endeavoured to secure the hall for another hour, but other and more worldly matters intervened. I think, then, we should let Egholm say what his conscience permits him, and then conclude with the old hymn: 'All is in the Father's hand.'"

"I should just like to ask Prophet Finck," said Egholm furiously, "how *he* would interpret and explain...."

"What's that?" said Finck loftily.

"The leading point, the essence of the whole thing, namely, the text found by me in the Epistle to the Hebrews—you have not said a word about that, really. I am firmly convinced that I am right, but, all the same, I should like to hear how you propose to explain away...."

"Write it down," broke in Finck sharply.

Egholm obeyed involuntarily. He found a stump of lead pencil in his waistcoat pocket, and began scrawling on the faded paper at the back of his Bible. He was a facile writer ordinarily, but in his present state of emotion he could hardly frame his question. Two or three times he struck out what he had written and began again. Suddenly he heard young Karlsen clearing his throat, and then:

"Now, then, we'd better...."

"No, no!" cried Egholm.

"Throw that man out," commanded Finck.

"You cowards, you're afraid to let me speak!"

"Oh, go and heave him out, Johannes," called young Karlsen, leaning over the footlights.

But Johannes, the postman, was paralysed already by the unwonted tumult, and did not move. There were others in the hall, however, who seemed eager enough to respond to the invitation, seeing that Karlsen himself was to be responsible.

"You miserable traitor," hissed Egholm, "give me back my tithes, give me my money, and I'll go. But not before. Give me my four hundred *kroner*."

"Turn him out, the wretch!"

"'All is in the Father's hand,
All things answer His command....'"

The Angel made a brave attempt to start the hymn, but the congregation appeared more interested in the conflict, and no one followed his lead.

"My money—give me my money, you thieves!"

"Pot calling the kettle black!" cried the Evangelist, with a sneer.

"Liar, slanderer, scoundrel!" roared Egholm, seeing in this last remark a reference to the manner of his dismissal from the railway service. And, beside himself with fury, he raised the heavy Bible to throw at Karlsen, when a diversion took place which drew off his attention and that of the audience.

A confused but violent noise came from the back of the hall, and then repeated shouts that rose above the din.

"You lanky black beast! You filthy devil! What about the seventh commandment? Yes; it's you I mean, you filthy, incontinent swine! You evangelical hypocrite! What about Metha, eh? She's lying there at home now and asking for you—for you!"

The words were plain and to the point; everyone in the hall stared in amazement at the backsliding photographer, who was standing on a bench and waving clenched fists in the air. It was evident that he had been drinking.

Then they turned to look at young Karlsen. His face was drawn awry.

Egholm was so moved at this unexpected reinforcement that the tears flowed down his cheeks. He found voice again and took up the cry.

"They're a lot of criminals, all of them. Setting themselves up against God's laws that I've discovered. I'll have you up, that I will. Give me my money, my money!"

Young Karlsen lost his self-control. He sprang in long leaps down through the hall, and flung himself upon Egholm, thrusting his head forward like a bull about to charge.

"You shut yo' jaw!" he cried, lapsing into his country dialect.

"Lauritz, be careful!" cried the Angel warningly. But it was too late. Finck came up to take part, and Egholm was borne towards the door, still shouting, and hanging on with arms and legs to the benches as he passed.

A little party of Brethren carried Meilby in similar fashion to the door. Serve him right, the sneak, always behindhand with his tithes….

The hall was filled with shouts and oaths, cries, and the barking of a dog.

The Histrionics gathered open mouthed about the doorway. It was their dress-rehearsal night for the coming performance of *The Lovers' Secret*.

VI

Meilby was in difficulties with his dress—his braces had given way—and Egholm was sucking an abrasion on the back of his hand. Nevertheless, each felt a sense of relief, as they walked briskly over the cobblestones, talking loudly and emphatically.

"If the Lord had sent a rain of fire upon their heads ... I was looking for it all the time. I can't understand that He didn't. Can you, now?"

Meilby answered, with a self-satisfied smile:

"Wasn't wanted, that's about it. He sent me instead."

"Yes; that's true. Thanks, Meilby—thanks for your help," said Egholm, pressing the other's arm. "But what was it all about, really? I was so excited at the time.... I mean, what was behind it all?"

"Ha ha, yes, what was behind it all! Metha Madsen was behind it all—Metha and her brat. Karlsen's it was, and they've been trying to make out it was mine."

"Terrible, terrible!"

"No; it's not. I'm going away, and I'll be out of it all. The old Angel in his little shop, he fixed it all up, for her to say it was me. Wouldn't have done for his dear little son, you know, and an Evangelist into the bargain. Kid was born at ten o'clock, and it wasn't stillborn either."

"But you could declare on oath...."

"Well, you know, that's a ticklish business. On oath.... No; I did the only thing there was to be done—came along every evening to the meetings, and glared at them, and threatened to kick up a scandal. But it's not so easy to make a speech in a crowd like that. Anyhow, I managed it all right this time, didn't I?"

"Splendidly. And now—you're going away?"

"To-morrow. First thing to-morrow morning," whispered Meilby hoarsely. "Come up with me now. I shan't go to bed to-night."

"Why, it's all empty!" said Egholm dismally, looking round the place. There was a travelling trunk in the middle of the studio floor, and that was all.

"Every rag and stick cleared out," said Meilby triumphantly.

"But you promised me—you promised me for certain...."

"Oh, I've fixed it up for you all right. Never meant to do you in, you know. That I swear. Not from the first evening. Here—here's the pawnticket for some neat little things—that's yours. I've sold the rest. Eh? Oh, don't mention it, not at all."

Egholm read the legend on the ticket—for a matter of a few *kroner* he could buy the camera thing outright. He was delighted; he was touched.

"None of your sneaking Angel ways about me," said Meilby simply.

"And what are you going to do over there when you get there?"

"How should I know? Don't even know where America is. If I hadn't got my ticket, I'd never find the way. But I've got it all right, thank the Lord! Here, you can see. Looks like business, doesn't it, what? But it's a long way, that's true. Wonder if there's women there...."

Egholm staggered off homewards.

If only he could go with Meilby. Get away out of this hole, with its hypocrites and scoundrels, its patent-shoed prophets and broadcloth deacons, away to America....

Yes; Egholm felt he must go. Not to America, of course—that was beyond him. But go somewhere. Just a few miles away. Knarreby, for instance, or somewhere thereabout. Meilby's camera would keep him above water, wherever he chose to commit himself to the waves—himself, that is. As for his family, well, he could always send some money home.

Anna was still up when he got back. He sat down and commenced telling her about the meeting. Also, that he was going away. He grew excited again, but she did not seem to take in all he was saying. There was something strange about her this evening....

"I knew it all along," was all she said.

She was still moving about when he rolled himself in the bedclothes and laid his weary head on the pillow. But suddenly a fresh quiver of raw pain went through her. She staggered to the bed and dropped.

"Oh ... Egholm, it's coming. You'll have to—go and fetch her now. You know where she lives...."

Beyond her pain and fear, she felt for one brief moment a blessed sense that this was *her* hour; she was to be the centre of importance for once. It was a victory.

Her husband, on his part, felt no share in anything victorious. He roused her quickly to her senses.

"It'll have to keep till to-morrow," he said in an offended tone. "You surely don't mean to send me running about now in the middle of the night?"

But it would not keep till to-morrow....

Egholm suffered considerably that night. A couple of women whom he did not remember to have seen before came up to assist the midwife, and took possession of the place, relegating him—the master—to the status of a slave. One handed him a bucket, indicating simply that it was to be emptied in the dustbin in the yard. He was not accustomed to such errands, but went down the dark stairs meekly. He had barely returned, when, shaken as he was, they bade him run at full speed to the chemist's. He looked round helplessly for Hedvig and Sivert, but the children had already been safely lodged with Eriksens' down below, out of the way. Egholm went. He took it like a man. True, he wept, but he did not scream aloud, as did his wife over her part.

Later on, towards morning, he was ordered to find some tape. As the simplest way of searching, he took his wife's workbox and tipped it upside down. He found no tape, but he found some crumpled letters, which interested him as soon as he perceived the signature was his own.

Egholm's features writhed themselves into expressions of disgust as he read the tender words, the ardent longing, with which he had once written to a certain "dearest Anna."

There were even some verses dedicated to that same Anna—"Dove of my heart...."

The verses in themselves were chiefly in praise of Helsingør, Helsingør.... As through a mist Egholm saw the two women who had played any part in his life—Clara Steen, from Helsingør, and Anna, from Aalborg. Once, the two had been as one in his mind—it was at the time he wrote those letters. The verses to Helsingør, dedicated to Anna, were proof of it. And now —ah, now ... Clara, a silken-soft, delicious dream, and Anna, a heavy, sighing, hollow-eyed reality.

Clara—what of Clara now? No; she was forgotten. All that Egholm remembered was the picture of her on the wall of her father's office. But he remembered that only too well. Though it was long now since he had seen it of nights....

Egholm, the weary, his night's rest broken, his hopes trampled under the butcher-boots of Karlsen Junior, his past for years back a ravening hunt for work; Egholm, the miserable, sank down on a chair and buried his face in the litter from the workbox, with the letters under it.

There was a bitterness in his mouth almost of physical disgust....

As it grew light he stole out of the house. The women were making coffee, with a great deal of fussing about. He seemed to remember they had come in once during the night, and showed him a child. He had expected it, and showed no surprise....

The walk out along the frosted roads did him good.

That money for the camera must be found. Ten *kroner*—after all, it was not a million. And he *must* have them....

He came back home warm and cheerful, to find the house in an atmosphere of rejoicing that fitted well with his mood.

Anna lay there in bed with a splendidly clean nightdress on, and a face younger by years.

"Did you ever see such a blessing of things?" she said, pointing round the room. "What do you think that is? *Butter!* And there's soup. Sit down, you poor thing. Hedvig, make haste and dish up a plate of soup. And Mother's sent ten *kroner*. Don't say the day of miracles is past!"

"Why, that'll pay for the journey!" Egholm exclaimed, with emotion.

"Journey? What journey?"

"Er—well, you remember.... We said before...."

"Oh no!" cried Anna, trembling. "You mustn't, Egholm. You mustn't. God's everywhere. He can help you here as well. I haven't been able to be much to you lately, I know, but only wait a little, and you shall see. With God's help, I'll be up and about again in four days from now. I can generally manage with four, you know.—Yes, I know you always say the gipsies and that sort don't need to stay in bed at all, but then they're more like animals than human beings—heathen, at any rate. Don't go away now, Egholm; you see how I'll work—oh, you wait and see. And make money, and you'll get work, too, all right."

"Never, in this beastly place."

"Yes, you will. Listen. Last night, when it was over, and the women had gone, I lay thinking of the lovely boy the Lord had sent me. I felt such a relief, and it was all so good and nice. It was about four, I think. And just as I was dropping off again, I saw a man with two bright eyes standing there by the cradle...."

"A spirit, you mean?" said Egholm, with a gasp.

"Yes, yes.—Be careful, you're spilling the soup. I lay there quite quiet, and looked at him, and he looked at me. I dared hardly breathe, for fear he should vanish again. His eyes were ever so big—and I can't tell you what a gentle look in them."

"Did he say anything?"

"He nodded several times, and then he said: 'That boy is sent to help you.' Oh, you can't think how lovely it was. When I woke up I could feel I had been crying."

"When you woke up—why, then, it was only a dream." Egholm was deeply disappointed.

"Dream? No; I wasn't asleep, only just dozing, I tell you. He stood there as plain and alive as you are now."

But Egholm went on with his soup. And he had his way. He was to go off that very day. Sivert was despatched to the pawnbroker's for the camera, and while he waited, Egholm was as gentle as could be. His wife could not remember having seen him so kind, not for years past. He took one of the snowdrops from the bedside—Hedvig, with her usual readiness, had stolen them from Eriksens' garden for her mother—and put it in his buttonhole.

"Good-bye, dear, and take care of yourself," said Egholm, and kissed his wife on both cheeks.

Anna was touched at so much gentleness. The tears flowed from her eyes.

VII

As Egholm came up to the station, he caught sight of young Karlsen. He was pale, and there was a cut on the bridge of his nose, but his temper was of the best.

"Aha!" he said artfully, nudging Egholm with his elbow. "Aha!" And he grinned.

That nudge, that grin, and that "Aha!" said much. They seemed to imply that Karlsen and Egholm had a pleasant—oh, a delightful little secret between them.

"A nice way you treated me last night," said Egholm. He would have spoken more forcibly, a great deal more forcibly, but his mind was distracted by the thoughts of his journey. He had not yet made his choice of where to go. And the world was wide. "I hadn't expected that of you—after what you said. You know."

"Let not the sun go down upon thy wrath. And—er—bless them that curse you, and—er—put up thy sword into its sheath, for.... Well, anyhow. You see, the old man wouldn't hear of it. It was no earthly good. He said he'd resign first. Put yourself in my place, my dear fellow. And then I began to be doubtful myself, too, afterwards, about it all. Come and have a drink. You look as if you were going off somewhere. What's on now?"

"Er—I'm going away," said Egholm nervously. "Going to open a photographic studio."

"Well, I never," said Karlsen, with ungrudging wonder. "And where's it going to be? You never said a word about that before."

"I had a studio once in Copenhagen—Østergade, a splendid position. And customers accordingly. Made any amount of money. This time I'm going to try—er—Knarreby. Quite a nice little place, don't you think?"

(There! Now it was said.)

"Knarreby? Oh yes, first-rate."

They went into the waiting-room. Egholm carried the camera himself, Sivert following behind him with the handbag.

"*Skaal*,[2] Egholm, and here's to burying the hatchet. Friends again now, aren't we? We were both a bit upset last night, and didn't know quite what we were doing. Turn the other cheek, what?"

"I was going to, only you were holding me behind."

"Ha ha! That's good. Taking it literally, as you might say. That's very good. *Skaal!* Have another of these. Yes; go on. I'm sure you can."

Egholm joined in the laugh at his own jest. Now that he had finally decided, all was brightness and freedom ahead. Away, away, like a bird that wakes to find its cage suddenly open. He could feel no anger against anyone now.

"Have a cigar," said Karlsen. There was no end to his amiability to-day.

"I don't smoke."

"Don't you, though? I say, Egholm, I wonder if you'd be above doing me a little favour?" Karlsen bit off the end of his cigar.

"Certainly, certainly." Egholm dived willingly into his pocket and pulled out a box of matches.

"Thanks—as a matter of fact, it wasn't matches so much I was thinking of. Another little matter...." The match flared and flared.

Egholm happened to glance at the other's face. The bright black eyes, with a fan of wrinkles out to the side, reminded him of fluttering cockchafers. Why, the man was nervous himself! His hand was shaking. And suddenly he brought the match too close to his beard....

"Of all the cursed.... H'm. Well, never mind.—Look here, Egholm, you couldn't manage to fix up another youngster at your place—a baby? You've quite a crowd already; it wouldn't be noticed. It's not mine—ha ha! No; it's Meilby's. I daresay he's told you.... Silly thing to do—playing with fire...."

"But why should I...."

"Ah, that's just where it comes in. In the first place, there's no one I'd sooner trust with a little angel like that, than you, my dear friends. And, in the second place, it'll be worth something to whoever takes it, and I'd like you to have the money. It'll be paid for, and well paid for. See what I mean?"

Egholm was alert in an instant. His heart was bubbling over with gratified malice. He put on a thoughtful expression as he took his ticket.

"Was it Meilby that put you on to me?"

"Well, yes and no. He comes to the meetings, you know, so I'd like to help him if I can. I can't take the kid myself, you understand. The mother's in a dairy all day."

"But about the money," said Egholm, moving towards the train. "What's it worth?"

"Oh, any amount," said the Evangelist. In his delight at finding Egholm so amenable to his plan, he forgot to restrain his play of feature. "Hundred and fifty *kroner* at the least. Let him pay, the beggar, it's his own fault, and I'll give him a talking-to. I went up to his place just now, by the way, but he wasn't in."

Egholm was in his seat. The train was ready to start.

"I'll tell you where he is," said Egholm, with a smile. "He's on his way to America by now. I said good-bye to him last night."

Young Karlsen was not used to being made a fool of. He collapsed as the train moved off; he waved a clenched fist furiously after it, and shouted. Then, turning to go, he discovered Sivert.

"What are you grinning at, you young devil?"

"He's forgotten his bag," said Sivert, shaking his white mop of hair with a satisfied smile.

But Karlsen found poor comfort in that.

VIII

Sivert stood in the smithy, trembling in every limb each time the hammer clanged on the iron plate. His mother had just gone, and he was alone. The hammer crashed like thunder, and he expected every moment to be struck by lightning.

"Look to your work," said the blacksmith.

Fru Egholm had shaken her head at first, when she saw there was a boy wanted at Dorn's smithy. Sivert a blacksmith? Never. But as there was no other job to be found in all Odense, and when Dorn explained that he wasn't a blacksmith really, but a locksmith and general metal worker, she agreed, albeit with some mistrust.

The boy stood holding a metal plate, his master cutting through it along chalked-out lines. It was to be a weathercock, in the shape of a horse. Suddenly—just at an awkward turn—the plate slipped, and the smith snipped off one lifted foreleg.

For a second or two he seethed like a glowing bar of iron thrust into water. A box on the ears was not enough....

"Here, Valdemar!" he cried to his man. "Take hold of the little beast, and we'll cut his fingers off. That's it. So!"

Sivert wriggled and screamed, and even tried to kick. But the man behind only crushed him the harder in his blouse-clad arms, till the boy's limbs hung limply down and his voice died to a hoarse gasp.

The smith opened the little white-knuckled hand with a grip as if shelling peas, and drew one finger between the shears, but managing carefully so that the boy could wrench it away at the critical moment.

This, of course, prolonged the joke, and made it all the funnier.

The man, too, began to find it interesting; his dull eyes glittered like molten metal newly set. There was a kind of anticipation in his mind—he realised that he would find considerable enjoyment in having Sivert all to himself when they went up to the bedroom they were to share at nights. It was but a vague thought as yet, a blind and pale Proteus moving uncertainly in the secret passages of his mind.

At dinner, while master and man sat over their porridge, Sivert was busy peeling potatoes for the next course. He sat on the wood box out in the kitchen, a tiny place, which was filled with the odour of Madam Dorn. She was the hugest piece of womankind Sivert had ever seen, and full of curious noises. Every other moment there came a threatening rumble from within like an approaching hurricane—perhaps she was hungry, too—then she would clear her throat with a thick, full sound, that seemed to rise from unknown depths. Sivert made the surprising discovery that her posterior part resembled a huge heart when she bent down. Was that perhaps an indication of general kindliness?

Now and again she came over to where he sat, and thrust her fingers down among the potatoes, to see if there were enough done yet.

It was a long, long time before the kitchen door opened, and the two superior beings within said, "*Tak for Mad.*"[3] Not till then could Sivert fall to upon the crumbs from their richer table—a draggled herring and a few diseased potatoes.

"It's a funny big world," thought Sivert, "but seems mainly alike in most things." His father's thrashings had been delivered with more solemnity than his present master's clouts, but then, on the other hand, Father would never have left a whole herring.

He had just finished washing up when the smith woke from his afternoon nap. "Kept up with him that time," thought Sivert, with some pride.

Evening came, after an endless day. Sivert had had his supper, and was standing with the bucket of leavings out by the pigs' trough, when he saw the journeyman striding out through the gate—a sight to see, with his hat down over his eyes and a cigar between his teeth pointing upwards. The boy wept with emotion at seeing him go—*that strangling brute.* Ah, the day was over now. He would have peace at last. He could go to bed.

The pigs sniffed at the empty bucket, and grunted encouragingly. Sivert was overjoyed with the pigs—he had made friends with them already, after dinner. There were two of them, one black.

He clambered up on the partition, and talked confidentially to them about the events of the day.

"Now, don't you think I'm crying, because I'm not. Not a bit of it. I promised mother I wouldn't. I was only wiping my nose, and you thought I was crying—ha ha, I did you there! And I'm not homesick, no; only making a little invisible sound, the same as when you're homesick. It's a trick I've learnt, and it's not everybody can do it. Just listen.... No; you've got to be quiet. You make worse noises than Madam Dorn. Homesick? What for, I should like to know? Father in Knarreby? I tell you I'm not fretting for him a single bit. Still, he couldn't do anything to me about the bag; he never said I was to put it in the train.

"Homesick? For Hedvig, perhaps? She's not really warm to sleep with, you know, and she always pulls the clothes off me. Oh, but of course you don't know Hedvig. She's my sister—a girl, you understand…."

Sivert realised on a sudden that between his knowledge and that of his hearers was a great gulf fixed. He fell to laughing, and then shook his head contemptuously.

"As like as not you don't even know what sort of thing a girl is at all. Poor silly pigs that you are. Now, I know all the things there are in the world. But I was stupid myself once."

A little before eleven he clambered up to the attic, his own bedroom, the one thing that had tempted him most of all when his mother had pointed out what he would gain by going out into the world, instead of staying at home.

"And you'll have your own room, with a big bed you can turn about in whenever you like and as much as you like, with no one to pinch you for being a nuisance. And you can cut out pictures and stick them up on the walls, and on Sundays you can pick flowers and put them in water to last all the week. And then when the mistress comes up to make the bed, she'll say: 'Why, what a nice lad we've got, now. Picking flowers….'"

He was much puzzled to find that there were *two* beds, and neither of them made. Mistress must have forgotten it. And what on earth was he to do with two beds? Perhaps the boy they had had before used to lie in one of them till it got warm; and then shift over to the other. That way, of course, you could keep them both warm. But…. No. Sivert decided not. Much better to save the wear of them, and only sleep in one. Mistress, no doubt, would appreciate that, and praise him for it.

He noticed, certainly, that there were some clothes on a chair, and a trunk between one bed and the window, but all unused as he was to the ways of out-in-the-world, he thought nothing of it. There were often things lying about at home here and there. After much consideration, he chose one of the beds, and sank to sleep.

Late that night came journeyman locksmith Valdemar August Olsen home, quite appreciably drunk. He stopped singing as he entered the gate, and took off his boots at the foot of the stairs, moved, no doubt, by some vestige of respect from his apprentice days.

He did not seem to need a light, but sat down on Sivert's bed, talking softly to himself. Suddenly he felt something alive under the bedclothes, and started up, almost sobered by the fright. He fumbled for matches, and a moment later was staring into the face of a pale, whitish-haired boy, who sat up in bed with wide, terror-stricken eyes.

Olsen waved the match till it went out, and threw away the stump. The boy must not see him quake. That bed there—it had been empty for three months past, ever since Boy Sofus ran away.

"Ha, frightened you, what?"

"Yes."

Olsen called vaguely to mind the interesting episode of the morning; he lit the lamp, and sat down again on the edge of Sivert's bed.

"No need to be frightened of me. I shan't hurt you."

He thrust his hand under the bedclothes, and stroked the child's knobby spine. It gave him a curious sensation, something promising and yet uncanny. He had felt like that once before, when he had bought a bottle of spirits for the night, but mislaid it.

Drowsy as he was, but still obstinate, he sat like a beast of prey, watching his time. Now and again he sniffed at Sivert's scalp—he had noticed the smell of it that morning when he was holding him.

"What d'you want to have long hair like that for?" he asked.

Sivert felt it would be dangerous to be at a loss for an answer. And, diving swiftly into the primeval forest growth of his mind, he snatched the first fruit that came to hand.

"That's for the executioner to hold on by, when he's cut off the body," he said.

"Executioner—what the devil!—cut off the body. It's the head that's cut off, stupid."

"Oh," said Sivert. "Not the body, then?"

But Valdemar August felt strangely confused in his mind. He tried again and again to see that curious question clearly, but in vain. Then he gave it up, and began talking at random of the days when he was out on his travels, after ending his apprenticeship, some ten years before.

He had passed through no end of towns, lodged in all sorts of places. He told of it all in short, descriptive sentences, always beginning with the words: "And then...."

"And then we came over to Jutland—and then we went down to Kolding—and then my mate said ... and then said I...."

He had set out on his travels with a receptive mind, and had seen and experienced much. It was not just ordinary things such as the position and "sights" of the different towns that had impressed him, but each place was associated with some new and remarkable experience, vicious for the most part, that came to his mind anew as soon as he named the scene.

Sivert dropped off to sleep for a second at a time, between the intervals of Olsen's recurrent "And then...." He understood but little of it all, but was grateful to find no immediate prospect of thrashing or strangling. If only he weren't so sleepy, and so horribly cold. And how long was it to last? Olsen was telling now of an inn where they had found a dead rat in a steaming dish of cabbage, and of how they had paid the host in his own coin.

He laughed at the joyous recollection, and nudged the boy in the ribs. His imagination grew more fertile, he used ever stranger words, until at last Sivert began to wake up, and feel amused. Evidently this Olsen was a merry soul, though it was hard to make him out at first.

Suddenly Olsen jumped up, and began dancing about in the half-dark in his ill-mended socks, making the queerest antics. Sivert took advantage of a burst of laughter to bury his tired head among the pillows, but a sudden silence made him open one eye warily and peer out into the room.

Olsen was standing over him, looking wilder and more incomprehensible than ever. Sivert was paralysed with fear. He was about to scream, but thought better of it—perhaps, after all, it was not so bad but that he could turn it off with a grin. And with an utmost effort, he broke into a fine imitation of a hiccuping laugh.

Then Olsen's rough hand closed over his mouth.

IX

What seemed most remarkable of all to Sivert was that there was never anything strange about Olsen's manner in the daytime, even when the smith was not there.

Olsen by day was simply brutal, like any ordinary man; his eyes, that glittered so insanely in the dark, looked out in daylight with a gleam of unadulterated cruelty from under the brow they shared in common. And the hand that stroked him so affectionately could land out a blow that would make his ears tingle all day.

For a time Sivert endeavoured to persuade himself that it was merely nightmare. But there were things that could not be so explained. And he bore his horror alone, for his mother misunderstood the hints he threw out, owing to the fact that Sivert, as was his custom, assured her that Olsen *did not* do so-and-so.

"I should think not, indeed. It's wicked even to think such things."

"But I can't help it."

"Then say your prayers properly and earnestly, and God will help you all right."

"I say my prayers like anything, every night. But Olsen's ever so strong, and it's no good. God can't manage him, I suppose."

"Sivert!"

"Or perhaps God doesn't trouble about things as much as people say."

"Sivert, now be a good child, do. Do you think God doesn't trouble about us? Why, look, what a lovely boy He's given us now...." Fru Egholm lifted the coverlet aside, to show the baby's face. "Isn't he sweet? And so healthy he looks. I think he'll be fair haired."

"But you promised me I was to be the only fair-haired boy?"

"I'd like to have as many of them as I can. They're the best sort. And, you know, Abel was fair haired, but Cain was dark."

"Just like Father!"

"Oh, child, how can you say such a thing!" Fru Egholm chattered on to cover her confusion. What a head the child had, to be sure.

The little one in the cradle awoke, and set up a faint cry like the bleating of a lamb. His mother took him up to her breast.

Sivert looked on with an expression of intense disgust.

"That's enough—that's enough," he said again and again, his eyes straining awry in consuming envy.

"Mother, let's break it up, let's tear it to bits, before it gets any bigger."

"What do you think your father would say to that?" said his mother, with a smile.

Sivert started; he had not thought of that difficult side of the question.

"Couldn't we say it had got lost somehow? No, I know; we'll tell him there never was but me and Hedvig. He won't remember. And then we can show him me, and ask if that's the one he means. Oh, may we, dear little darling mother?" And he stretched out his hand for the child.

"Just listen and I'll tell you what Father says," said his mother, feeling in a pocket of her dress.

Sivert's face darkened; he stared anxiously at the letter.

> "MY DEAR ANNA,—Excuse my long silence, but I have got things settled now, and every day feeling happier for the change. Karlsen, the Evangelist, has been a nightmare to me, but now I am awake once more, and drink in the fresh air and feel myself another man. And only fancy—*my powers of invention*, that I thought were dead, have come back again stronger than before. You remember I used to say I was as *the hand of God* here on earth. I am to go over the work, file away at it and make it even— in a word, *improve the whole world*, that He created great and rich and round, it is true, but rough at the edges. In my innermost self, and right out to my fingertips, I feel conscious of this as my calling. If I only go for a little walk with the wind against me, I feel my powers in urgent movement. Now, the friction exerted by the wind could be reduced to one-seventh by means of a little invention of mine. I can tell you, there is a *great time* ahead. But it is not this that occupies my mind just now, but something else. A machine. I dare not set down on paper what it is. Only this: be sure that all the taps and other parts of the *steam wagon*, my old construction, are sent to me here as soon as possible. I must try my wings now; I feel myself free. Free as a bird."

"So I should think," murmured Fru Egholm. "With no wife and children or anything else to look after. Well, thank goodness that's not all."

"I believe God Himself has led me to this place, and guided my footsteps in the way."

"Yes, I daresay—but who was it went down on her knees a hundred times and prayed God to deliver you out of that Angel creature's claws?"

Fru Egholm knew the letter by heart from end to end. Nevertheless, each line affected her now as strongly as if read for the first time. Even then, despite her critical opposition to the present passage, she was already feeling for her handkerchief, ready for the touching part she knew was just ahead.

"I have fitted up a splendid little studio in a carpenter's place. Do you think anyone in Odense would ever have given me credit for the rent, and paid for a glass roof into the bargain and all that? When I came into the town the first day, it was like a triumphal march. I walked down from the station with a man, and asked him if he knew a place where I could put up. 'Yes,' said he; 'you can stay at Vang's hotel. My name's Henrik Vang; it's my father owns the place.' I shook my head, thinking of my 3 *kroner* 50 that was all I had. But he said I could fix my own price; he'd look after that all right. Did you ever hear of such luck? We spent the whole evening together, in the restaurant, and all the notables of the town were there. He told them to put it all on his bill. While I think of it —be sure to send my embroidered waistcoat and the small boots, if you can manage it. They're only in for a small sum, and you should be able to get them out all right, now you haven't got me to feed...."

"Only a small sum! Heh! Embroidered waistcoat and creaky boots—no, my good man, you won't get them, and that's flat."

But now came the part that filled Fru Egholm with joy and pride. Egholm wrote that he had been thinking much about the vision she had had on the night the child was born. It would be as well to give the child a name that should remind the Lord of His promise. He would suggest *Emanuel*.

Was there ever such a thoughtful creature in the world? And it was the first time Egholm had ever troubled himself to think of a name for any of the children. But perhaps he was a different man now. For he wrote further:

"The country round here is lovely. Only two minutes' walk from my studio down to the shore. Might easily have a little sailing boat there, all ready to hand. I often go down there, but only for a minute at a time—there might be people coming up while I was out. You must see and come over soon. I am longing for you, dearest Anna...."

"And I'm longing, too," said Fru Egholm, using her handkerchief. "Man and wife should be one, as they say. But what about you young ones? Hedvig ought surely to be able to get a place in Knarreby, no worse than the one she's got. It's you that's the trouble, Sivert lad."

"Olsen's a good enough hand at thrashing, but I think Father beats him at using hard words," said Sivert judicially.

The matter was not one to be settled out of hand. Money was not the only difficulty. Fru Egholm had gradually worked up quite a decent business connection with the sewing of grave-clothes. One day she had made 1 *kroner* 67 *øre, net earnings.* And a business like that was not to be lightly thrown away.

Hedvig was getting on nicely, at school and in her situation, and Sivert's curious revelations grew less frequent.

Indeed, the boy suffered less now from the attentions of his tormentor at the smithy than at first. There were always the wonderful stories to begin with, and these he took as a kind of compensation for what followed. Olsen had also a book which he would bring out on rare occasions. It was a crumpled rag to look at, from the outside. But within were marvels. Sivert's eyes glowed when Olsen took it out of the drawer. It was his journeyman's book, at once a passport and a register.

Page after page, the stamp and signatures of the police—the State Authorities, no less. One stamp for every imaginable town.

Sivert was dumb with emotion. Even Olsen's voice shook. And in the middle of showing it, he would sometimes snatch up the book with an oath and hide it jealously against his naked breast, only to draw it forth lovingly a moment later. It was as if he could not bear the glorious vision for more than a little glimpse at a time.

It was a treasure of almost inconceivable value, was that book. Better to lose one's own head than that, for, once lost, the unfortunate owner would be put in prison on the spot. On the other hand, whoever held such a book, duly stamped and signed and in order, might wander the whole world over, and none should dare to touch a hair of his head.

In the front of the book was something more wonderful even than the police stamps. Sivert had been three times granted a sight of it. Nothing less than a painting in words of the owner of the book. The boy grew giddy at the thought that in five years' time he, too, might attain a like distinction.

"Height—58 inches.
Hair—black.

Eyes—brown (eyebrows meeting in centre).
Nose—ordinary."

Sivert turned his eyes from the book to the living Olsen before him; it was a marvel that anyone could have hit off the description thus to a hair.

But then came the best of all:

"Any distinctive marks: *Has six toes on each foot.*"

Olsen threw back his head, and set his lips sternly. Yes, he had six toes; it was perfectly true. And why shouldn't he? What, didn't believe it? Well, then, look here!

Off came Olsen's socks, and Sivert, in humble amazement, counted the whole dozen. True, the outermost toe was no giant, but rather a tiny blind thing that clung to the next. There was no nail to it, yet it was undoubtedly a toe. A whole limb additional!

Sivert counted his own inferior equipment again and again by night, and in course of time developed a fine gift of counting them wrong.

"Why don't they write down about your inside?" he ventured to ask.

"They can't. That's private," answered Olsen.

X

Henrik Vang loved a soft, easy seat, and from his very first visit he had chosen to sit down in the middle of Egholm's iron bed. Sometimes, when it was cold, he would pull the bedclothes up over his legs, right to his throat. Egholm did not mind. He preferred to walk up and down the floor, listening to his own voice. It was rarely but he had some new strange plan or invention in his head.

To-day, however, he was nervous, and void of ideas. Anna was coming by the midday train. Consequently, he found nothing now to talk of but old, worn-out themes. Of the Brethren, who had cheated him out of all that money. Of his great Day of Reckoning with those same Brethren, and how they had risen up and cast him forth, together with one Meilby, a photographer.

"He was something like you, Vang, by the way, was Meilby. Same light hair, and eyes—and especially in the look of them. Now, anyone not seeing that great big body of yours would say you weren't grown up yet. But Meilby, he was younger, and not so heavy built, perhaps."

"Was he married?"

"No, but he...."

"Then he wasn't like me."

"Ha ha—but he was, though, on my word. The voice, too. Same rumbling sort of way, as if that wasn't properly set either."

"Anyhow, he wasn't married, so he wasn't like me. She's been talking to Father again. Asking him to turn me out. I don't know if she wants me to die of hunger. For she never gives me anything herself."

"Well, you know, Vang," laughed Egholm, "you're not exactly a model husband, either. Women like being made a fuss of now and then. Now me, for instance. Here's my wife coming to-day, and what do I do? Go up to the station myself to meet her. See?"

Egholm looked at his watch, and felt uncomfortable. Again he had forgotten the time. The train must be in by now, and Anna would be left standing there, utterly strange to the place....

He left Vang in the nest he had made, and hurried out.

Annoyance at the little misfortune was but a herald for the host of black thoughts that had been gathering in Egholm's mind ever since the day when, in a weak—a very weak—moment, he had written to Anna to come.

Now, was it nice, was it decent of her, to take advantage of a momentary lapse like that?

Anyhow, it was too late now. The thing was done. Good-bye to freedom—he had himself turned back to seek his fetters. Anna would be there, right enough, standing on the platform ready to clap the handcuffs on him once more.

And now, just as things were beginning to move! With a wife and two hungry children to drag about after him, it would be stagnation once more, however he might put his shoulder to the work.

The gravel path leading to the station had been newly planted with trees, poor, scraggy things, more like the brooms on the buoys outside the harbour. And now they had to feel about with their roots through the hard earth. It would be ages before they grew to be tall and strong, with broad leafy crowns. And they were young—but he was no longer young, and his strength had been wasted in many a barren soil.

Egholm clasped his hands under his cloak, and prayed:

"Lord, spare Thy servant. Take away this cup from me. Let it be so that, when I come to the station, I may wake up out of a painful dream. No wife and children at all. Lord, hear Thy servant; hear him for that he suffered for the sake of Thy word, at the hands of the Brethren in Odense!"

He writhed his bony fingers, and looked up to the blue March sky. How grateful he would be; how he would fall down and bend his forehead to the earth, if his prayer should be heard!

But, alas, they would surely be there—Anna, Sivert, and Hedvig. Yes; they would be there, never fear.

It suddenly occurred to him that he could not remember the children's faces. All he could call to mind of Hedvig was her keen grey eyes, and Sivert was associated chiefly with the grating sound of a little saw. But that sound was so vividly present in his mind that he lashed out with his stick, by way of relief. It was a reflex movement, a case of cause and effect.

Egholm had expected to find his family on the steps of the station, but there was no one there. The whole place looked dead and deserted. The omnibus horse stood drowsing in its tether, while the driver, Red Jeppe, jested with the waitress at the bar. No one on the platform but a group of girls. And it was already half-past twelve by the clock.

Strange—very strange.

He drifted up to a porter, and asked:

"The train from Odense—has it come in yet?"

"She's broken down at Aaby. A nasty mess."

"Broken down!"

"Yes. Engine off the line, and...."

Oh! Egholm felt a nasty blow at his heart. So God—or was it Satan?—had heard his prayer for once. With an ashy face he asked again:

"Nobody hurt, I hope?" And the answer seemed to flash on him as a vision: Anna stretched out on a canvas bier, her thick hair matted with blood.

"Hurt? Oh, Lord, no," said the porter. "Only the engine turned off down the wrong track, and stuck in the gravel." He yawned hungrily. "You're not the only one hanging about here waiting for their blessed trains...."

Egholm felt a strange weakness in the legs, and sat down. The signal bell rang—train due in ten minutes. It seemed to him as if the station had suddenly brightened up. Quite cheerful all at once. Those girls there, for instance, with lovely new boots on. And laughing all the time. The one on the outside leaned right over to listen when the others whispered. Well, well, a good thing everyone wasn't miserable.

And there—there was a man coming out of the waiting-room—a tall, fat man with rather thin legs—a commercial traveller. He didn't look pleased at all, but dragged at his two bags like a convict in irons. Then, at sight of the girls, he stopped and drew himself up, anxious to be seen.

He draws a mirror and a tiny brush from his pocket, and wields them like a virtuoso. Then a cigar-case, and next a smart little contrivance for cutting off the end; another little case, with matches in. Evidently he is trying to impress those girls with an idea that he is a sort of original chest of drawers, with all manner of cases and shiny, interesting things inside. And he succeeds. The girls stop talking, and look at him, to see what will happen next. But after a little they fall to laughing again.

When the train rolled in, Fru Egholm, standing at the window of a compartment beyond the end of the platform, saw her husband come running down the length of the carriages, eagerly, with delighted eyes.

Hurriedly she took leave of a couple of women fellow-travellers. They had lived together for the past three or four hours, and suddenly that was over....

Egholm clambered up on the footboard, and found a pleasant surprise.

Sivert was not there!

True, there was little Emanuel, whom he had forgotten altogether for the moment. But then Emanuel was the child of victory. Or at least it was reasonable here, as ever, of two evils to choose the lesser.

Anna was a little puffy and dark under the eyes, but her cheeks were flushed with excitement. She and Hedvig handed out an endless array of packages, a lamp, some pictures, and the family treasure—the cut-glass bowl. One of the parcels was soft and round, and Anna proffered it with a warning:

"Be careful; don't lay it down anywhere. There might come a dog...."

Egholm fingered it over, and made out the contours of a fowl. His heart softened. And then, as Anna stood feeling helplessly behind her with her lace boots, he took her in his arms, helped her out, and twisted her round. Her face was flushed with confusion. The features he cared for hid those he hated. For a second he read the anxious questioning in her eyes, then a wave of deep sympathy overwhelmed him, and he pressed her to him again and again.

"I'm so glad you've come, Anna, my dear, I'm so glad."

Omnibus-Jeppe was to take the heavier luggage that was in the van.

"H'm," said Jeppe, scratching the back of his head, "there's enough to stock a shop."

Egholm scratched his head likewise, and stared helplessly at the bundles of bedding and Anna's flower-pots—a whole score of them.

"What on earth d'you want to drag all that about for?" he asked irritably.

"Oh, look! They've broken the calla there," wailed Fru Egholm, kneeling down beside it. "Broken right down at the root. And it was just coming out...."

"Oh, never mind that!"

"Give me a twenty-five øre, and I'll look after the lot," said Jeppe, melting at once before feminine grief.

The family had as much as they could carry. Egholm walked with pictures under either arm; his wife took the fowl, the cut-glass bowl, and the flower-pot with the calla. Leave it—because it was broken? No, she could never be so cruel.

Emanuel's perambulator lay upside down, revealing the advertisement placard for somebody's beer that had been tacked over the hole in the bottom. Hedvig tipped it right side up. It would hold a good deal, being of a peculiarly low, broad shape. Emanuel was ultimately placed among the various goods there disposed, as one surrounded by trophies in a triumphal car. He sat looking round with big blue eyes under his little white cap. It was a girl's cap, really—a sort of sunbonnet that had lain in a drawer since Hedvig's time, but —*Herregud!* what did it matter? At his age....

Egholm walked in front, the pictures waving up and down like a pair of wings as he described the view with great enthusiasm to his wife.

The slow-moving flood of the Belt glittered in newborn sunlight. The fields lay green and open under God's sky. The landscape looked one freshly and boldly in the eyes—Anna marked how the very air tasted utterly different from that about Eriksens' sour little patch of yard and garden. Her husband voiced her thought exactly when he said:

"I don't believe there's a prettier spot in all the world."

"But the town?" she asked in surprise. "Where is it?"

"Right up there in the bay. See the red church-tower there, and the Custom House—that yellow place standing out against the great black woods? The town's as sheltered as a bird in its nest. And look, that's Jutland over there—see how close it looks, and the two lines of coast all soft against each other. Looks almost as if they were dancing."

"And look at the white sails on the blue water!"

"Yes. I know that one with the topsail. That's Etatsraad Brodersen's. You know, 'Brodersen's Pure Grape.' He's the great man of the town."

"It's a lovely place."

"Ah, but wait till it's summer, and the beeches are out," said Egholm, with bright eyes. "We'll go out one day together. I'll show you it all."

Tears welled up into Anna's eyes. What a marvellous place was this Knarreby, that could so change her husband altogether! Actually running down the platform to meet them as if it had been visitors of rank. And no grumbling or scolding because the train was late.

Egholm was himself moved. He blinked his eyes and looked away.

Out on the Belt, Brodersen's cutter was cruising about. It was on the water early this year. There—it was tacking now. Stood for a moment straight as a white church, and then off on the new tack. Heavens, how it heeled over! Why don't they let go the sheet? Ah, there she was up again! But Egholm had somehow slipped out of his former joyous mood, and said a trifle absently and wearily:

"Yes, it's a pretty place; that's true."

Fru Egholm did not notice his altered tone. She found the moment opportune to put in a word for one that had been left behind in Odense, one that had stood on the platform in the early morning, waving and waving, till he suddenly collapsed, as if the ground had been snatched from under his feet. Was he not to have a share in the promised land?

"Sivert sent his love. He couldn't come, of course, poor child."

"No, thank goodness!"

The mother started—it was the old voice again. Her rejoicing had hurried her forward along a path that ended in a morass—she must drag her steps back now, uncertain of her way.

Listlessly she followed Egholm's account of some excursion of his own.

"We came round the point to an island that was like a floating forest—Heireøen, it's called. We put in there, alongside a pavilion place, and had steak and onions."

"Wasn't it dreadfully expensive—at a place like that?" Anna's voice was dull and joyless as her own meals and the children's had been every day, Sundays and weekdays alike, as far back as she could remember.

"I don't know. It was Henrik Vang that paid. That is to say—he knew the man who kept the place, and so...."

"Henrik Vang? Oh, that'll be the one you wrote about. His father's got a little eating-house or something."

"Little eating-house! Good Lord!—the finest hotel in the place. First-class restaurant!"

Anna had no grounds for disapproval, but, none the less, she murmured:

"H'm. A fellow like that...."

The family had reached the outskirts of the town. As they walked on, curtains were moved aside, and a nose-tip here and there showed through. In the little shops, the shopkeepers dropped their paper bags and crowded with their customers to see.

Hedvig enjoyed being thus a centre of attraction. She arranged the newspaper-holder, the plaster figure, and the lamp in a specially attractive fashion, drew herself up, tossed her head, and only wished they might have to walk all through the town. As it happened, she was disappointed.

Egholm, whose fingers were getting sore with holding the pictures, tripped on faster.

"There—that's where I live," he said, out of breath. "Pick up your legs a bit, can't you?"

"Where?"

"The grey house there, with the gateway."

All else was forgotten now in the anxiety to see the place that was to be their home. It was a long, low house. A gateway, two narrow shop-windows, a door, and four pairs of windows beside. Over the entrance was a placard inscribed with black letters on a white ground: "*H. Andreasen. Coffins and Funeral Furnishings.*"

A very respectable house it was, plastered with cement. And now they could see the show-case on one side of the entrance, with the photos in. No dream, then, no misunderstanding. It was here they were to live.

"Lord, isn't it fine!" cried Hedvig.

Anna sighed resignedly, even perhaps in relief.

Saw and plane stopped suddenly. The men wiped the cobwebs from the panes and looked out, their bare arms gleaming against their blue overalls.

Anna hurried in through the entrance, but stopped inside, and looked back at her husband inquiringly.

There was someone in there! She could feel it, and it made her ill at ease. She was ready to drop as it was, from weariness, and longed to hide herself between four walls, to get her breath in peace, and set about to make things comfortable for her husband, the children, and herself.

"What are you waiting for? Go along in—the door's open."

"But there's someone ... I thought I...."

"Oh, that'll be Vang, I suppose," said Egholm, opening the door himself. "Hullo, Vang, here we are again. Nobody been, I suppose? No, no. Well, here's my little party."

Vang was seated in the middle of the bed, with his hat on, and a cold cigar at one corner of his mouth. The bed had sunk under the weight of his heavy frame; the dirty sheets and spotted blankets were twirled up as by a waterspout.

"My husband wrote about you," Fru Egholm stammered with an effort. She stood holding her flower-pot and her parcels as if dreading to soil the paint of table and seats.

"Him and me," said Vang in a solemn bass, letting his chin fall forward on his chest—"him and me we've been as one. But I'm going now, all right."

"Why, what for?" said Egholm, touched. "There's no need...." He took Vang's arm.

"Ah, but I must. Henrik Vang can't stay where there's women about."

"What's turned you so serious all at once?"

Vang smoothed the bedclothes, evidently embarrassed.

"It's not just making a fuss, to be asked again. I know I'd rather stay. Where should I go to, anyway?"

"You've a charming wife at home," said Egholm mischievously. "But stay here if you like. I'll be only too pleased."

"Home? I'd rather walk in water up to my neck the rest of the day. But if you really mean it—if you'll let me stay where I am—still as a mouse, and never disturb a soul, why, I'd just love it."

"Do, then, Vang, do."

Vang turned with a smile towards Fru Egholm, who was removing her hat in silence at the farthest corner of the room.

"I'll stay, then, just as I am, in what I've got on. My clothes aren't much, anyway. And I'm mostly drunk as well. But when you get to know me, *Frue*, you'll see that right down inside I'm the man I am. Son of Sofus Vang. First-class hotel, excellent cuisine, and choicest wines—with terrace overlooking the water!"

Hedvig burst out laughing. She and her mother began carrying in the things Omnibus-Jeppe had piled up outside.

Egholm saw how he and Vang were gradually being immured behind the various belongings. It even seemed to him that now and then something was thrust with unnecessary harshness against his legs, and a threatening look crept into his eyes. In the midst of a flow of speech addressed to Vang, he broke off suddenly, and said in a voice of command:

"Take that stuff into the other room!"

"I will, dear. Let me," said Fru Egholm. "But it looked like rain, you know."

"Not that door," said Egholm angrily.

"But these are the kitchen things." Fru Egholm had already seen that the other door opened into an attic or box-room or something of the sort. "Isn't that the kitchen there?"

"Kitchen! That's my dark-room." Egholm spoke as might a God to whom creations are the merest trifle. The place might have been a kitchen. Well and good—Egholm spoke the words: "Let there be a dark-room."

"You'll have to manage in there—at any rate, for the present." He nodded towards the nondescript apartment opposite. "Make that a kitchen."

"But, my dear...." Fru Egholm pulled herself together with a poor attempt at a smile. Then she shook her head; it was hopeless to try to explain to the uninitiate what a little world in itself a kitchen is. "The stove...." she managed to protest. "There's not even a heating-stove in there."

She waited still, with the chest of utensils in her hands, before the forbidden door. She *must* get in there.

Egholm reflected that it was perfectly true about there being no stove. It was for that reason he had had his bed in here for the winter. He could find no way out of the difficulty, and grew furious—for even he was not so far almighty as to create a kitchen where no kitchen was.

"All right, get along with you, then?" he said, pushing her in, and Hedvig, with Emanuel in her arms, behind her. "There you are! But mind! No fooling about with any of my things!"

The door opened with a queer sucking noise—it had been caulked with strips of cardboard and cloth.

Hedvig and her mother stood aghast, while Egholm thrust past them and began moving his bottles with the easy familiarity of habit.

All the windows were darkened but one, that glared red as a furnace door. They could see nothing save their own hands, which looked strange and uncanny in the red light.

"Egholm, you surely don't mean to say we're to do the cooking here? When you can't see your hand before your face!"

Egholm stepped across and shut the door behind them; then, turning to his wife, he brought his face close down to hers, and whispered in a voice that seethed like a leak in an overheated boiler:

"Look here! You're not going to come along and ruin the business for me now, so don't you think it. If I can see to do my developing, you can see to cook. You understand?"

And he went on with a further flow of words, furious, though subdued.

Fru Egholm writhed.

"But, Egholm ... there's no *room*! I can't even see the stove.... Oh...."

She still clung to a faint hope that he might be brought to see things with her eyes, and realise how unreasonable it was to ask her.

"Very well. I'll give you a lamp. My dark-room lamp should be about here somewhere."

His fingers moved among rattling bottles on the stove.

"Here it is—no. Now, where the devil...."

A bottle upset; he grasped at it hurriedly and knocked over another; the liquid gurgled out into a pool on the floor.

"A basin—quick, give me a basin! My silver nitrate ... quick, a basin!"

They reached about for one in haste and confusion.

"Open the door so we can see!" cried Hedvig. But at the same moment her father came towards them. His face looked as if smeared with blood in the light from the red-covered pane; his teeth showed between parted lips.

"You—you're the serpent in the garden!" he hissed.

"Oh, don't!" she cried, her voice rising to a scream.

Emanuel was beginning to cry. Hedvig tried to wriggle through with him to the door, but stepped on the basin her father had just set on the floor.

This was too much for Egholm. He felt he must either discharge the current within, or be fused by it, like an overcharged wire.

He staggered one step back, then forward again. His arms rose up as if with an inner force of their own; then with his full strength he struck his clenched fist in his wife's face.

Once again, and once again he struck, the flesh of her checks squelching under the blows. Then he stumbled out, and closed the door carefully behind him.

Vang was seated on the bed exactly as before. What could he say to him? It was the first time any stranger had witnessed a scene of this sort. What was the use of starting upon heart-rending explanations, which Vang would never understand? And how much of the trouble had been audible through the close-padded door?

Vang gets to his feet; he must go now—yes, he must. There is something cowed about him; he speaks in a low voice, and does not look up. And Egholm, suddenly aware of Anna's sobbing and Hedvig's uncontrolled blubbering plainly heard through the door, realises that Vang must have been able to follow the drama through all its painful details.

And now he is going off, convinced that Egholm is a cruel, cruel brute.

It must not be! Egholm feels now, more strongly than ever before, that he *can* be so good, so good!

"No, no; you mustn't go!" he cries, as Vang steps cautiously over the bath full of flower-pots. He grips him by the arm, anxious to prove his all-embracing affection on the spot. "You mustn't go now I'm in all this mess. Didn't you say we'd been as one together? Wait a bit; there's something I want to talk to you about."

Egholm sat down on a ragged mattress, and covered his face with his hands.

If only he had something—some precious gift—to offer Vang. But he had nothing—not a copper *øre* in his pocket; not a thing. Not so much as a bite of bread for himself, still less for Vang. And what about the others?...

The fowl! The thought of it seemed to flow like something rich and soft and fat right out to his fingers. He straightened himself up and looked round —yes, there it was, in the perambulator.

"I was going to ask you to supper, Vang. My wife's brought a fowl along, a fine fat bird, almost as big as a drake. But I suppose you've something better for supper yourself?"

He gauged Vang's hunger by the rumbling of his own empty paunch, and made every effort to persuade him.

"A fine bird, a delicious bird; the size of a drake as nearly as can be."

Egholm was not quite sure whether a duck or a drake would be the larger, but took the word as it came into his head, to help him in his need.

Vang could not resist. He smacked his lips, and said:

"I could go down to Father's place, of course. They can't refuse me anything there, after all, though they do keep me waiting and make things as uncomfortable as they can. If only I could be sure your wife wouldn't mind...."

"Not a bit, not a bit," said Egholm cheerfully, relieved that all was well again. He had been cruel, by an unfortunate chance, but now he had wiped that out. Briskly he took up the parcel with the delicious bird, and even played ball with it as he went towards the dark-room door. The business in there before sickened him unspeakably.

There was a moment of deadly silence as he opened the door, but hardly had he taken a step forward when he ran against a shadow that would not let him pass. Next moment he felt Hedvig's skinny hands like claws, one at his chest, the other gripping his throat, as she hissed out:

"You dare to touch Mother again—you dare! Quick, Mother, take Emanuel and run!"

Egholm was more astonished than angry at first. What was all this?

But—ugh! it hurt! He tried in vain to wrest her hands away; then he struck at her head. But she ducked down between his arms and butted him over against the stove.

"Run—run quick! I've got him!"

"Let go, you little devil!—oh, help! she's strangling me!"

"Hedvig, what are you doing?—Hedvig, dearest child! Let go, do; it's your father!" Fru Egholm tried to pull her off.

Then Hedvig realised that the day was lost. She loosened her hold, and let Mother and Father wrest an arm to either side, till she stood as if crucified up against the wall, her head drooping, and yellow wisps of hair falling over her flushed face. And she fell to crying, with a horrible penetrating wail.

Egholm had still by no means recovered from his astonishment. He coughed, and began rubbing his neck, speculating the while on some appropriate punishment for the presumptuous girl.

"Well, you're a nice little beast, you are," he said. But he could hardly find more to say. There were not actually words in the language for criminals of that sex.

"You overgrown hobbledehoy, falling upon your own father, your own flesh and blood. I never heard of such a thing. If you had your deserts, you'd be bundled off to gaol this minute, you disgraceful young scoundrel."

Suddenly he began tearing down the planks and cardboard from the window, without a word of explanation, but with emphatic jerks and crashes that fell in time to his words and gave them added weight.

"You wait—I shan't—forget, you—squat-nosed—little—guttersnipe."

But for every tug at the flimsy covering, the light poured in more violently, like a wonderful grace of God. Both Hedvig and her mother, despite their indignation, could not help craning their necks to look, as the corner of a garden, with budding trees, came moving, as it were, towards them. Even Emanuel opened his eyes wide, and lifted his little hands towards the light.

Once he had begun, there seemed no end to Egholm's willingness to oblige. He cut the string by which the door was fastened, and tore away the padding from all sides.

"There! *Now*, are you satisfied?" he asked, with great politeness.

But there was something wanting yet to render his wife's satisfaction complete. Those bottles.... All along the shelves and dresser were rows of bottles, in every shape, thickness, and colour. Many of them were ticketed with complicated chemical names, and some bore the awe-inspiring death's-head poison label. Egholm had strung a tangle of lines from wall to wall, on which his photos hung to dry, exactly as when Hedvig played dolls' washing-day.

And the kitchen table was a veritable map of stains.

"They cost something, those did," said Egholm. "That's my silver nitrate." And he seemed as proud as if he had paved the way for his wife's arrival with pieces of eight.

He helped to set the numerous bowls and glass plates aside, and murmured regretfully:

"Well, well, anyhow, you've had your way."

"Yes, but...."

"I hope you can see now, at any rate. And now, for Heaven's sake, make haste and get that fowl done. I've asked Vang to supper."

"But, Egholm! You don't mean to say...." Fru Egholm almost screamed.

"Beginning again, are you?" he said threateningly. But at sight of her face, bruised and already colouring from his recent blows, he turned away.

"We must do something for him. He's been a help to me from the first day I came. And he's got a miserable home."

"We've neither knives nor forks—we haven't even plates." Fru Egholm dared not say too much just now, but hurried to unpack a box, that the contents might speak for her. There were a few cups without handles, five or six plates, some of them soup-plates, but no two alike. One had a pattern of flowers, another birds; a third was ornamented with a landscape. Two of the knives lacked handles, and nearly all the forks were one prong short.

"There! I don't know what you think?"

Egholm was on the point of breaking out again, but suddenly he laughed.

"Oh, an elegant dinner service. Splendid! splendid!" And he danced about the floor.

"We haven't a single dish, or a tureen. And his father keeps a real hotel

—we can't serve it up in the saucepan."

"Oh yes, you can. Vang and I, we're not the sort to stand on ceremony. Wait a minute, though—a dish ... I can let you have a dish."

He picked up a big white rinsing-dish from among his own equipment, fished up some plates that were lying in the bottom, and tipped the liquid into a bottle.

"There you are—real porcelain. Now the set's complete. But mind you wash it out well, or you'll send us all to kingdom come. And, for Heaven's sake, make haste. I've got to keep talking to him all the time, and you've no idea what a business that is."

Whereupon Egholm danced out of the doorway, leaving his wife, confused and helpless, with the dripping poison dish in her hands.

XI

Hedvig sat in front of the stove, crumpling up newspapers and thrusting them in through the open door, to keep the fire from going out entirely.

"This will never do," said her mother, wringing her hands. Egholm was tramping up and down in the next room, stopping every now and then to open the door and ask if the supper wasn't nearly ready. His face was pale—he was always most dangerous when he was hungry.

"Huh! Let them wait," said Hedvig.

"Run outside, dear, and see if you can't find some bits of something—a piece of board or some twigs or anything that'll burn. I fancy I saw some stuff under that bush in the corner."

Hedvig was always happiest when she found a chance of using her legs. She explored the yard across and across, quartering like a hound in all directions, and finding not a little in the way of fuel. When she had filled her apron, there was a knocking at one of the windows. At first she tried to ignore it, and was hurrying in with her findings, but the knocking was repeated, and more loudly. She turned angrily and looked in.

A brown-eyed young workman in the carpenter's shop stood beckoning to her, both hands full of beautiful lumps of newly cut wood.

This was a language Hedvig understood; she picked up her heels and ran to the workshop door.

"You the photographer's?" he asked, with a bashful grin and a slight lisp in his voice, as he laid the blocks like an offering in her apron.

"Yes," said Hedvig. "We haven't had time to get in any wood as yet. Mother and I only came to-day. We're going to have chicken soup for dinner. There's visitors."

"But what are the bones for?" said the man, picking about among the contents of the apron.

Hedvig flushed, but, ready witted as ever, answered, laughing:

"Oh. Perhaps you don't do that here. In Odense we always use bones for the fire when we can get them. They burn almost better than wood."

"What's your name?"

"Hedvig Egholm. And what's yours? You're the carpenter's son, I suppose?"

"No, I'm only working here, that's all. My room's just at that end—like to come and see it?"

"No, thanks. I must make haste in."

"Well, then, come this evening, or to-morrow. Will you?" he asked eagerly, routing about in all the corners for more wood.

But Hedvig only laughed, and shook her heavy yellow plaits. She came back to her mother with a load that reached to her chin. There was no need to use the bones, after all—they burnt well enough, it is true, but stank abominably in the burning.

Emanuel was given a row of the neat wooden blocks, set up on the table before him.

"Look—there's the puff-puff," said Hedvig.

The child laughed all over his face, but a moment later he was nibbling at the engine.

In the next room Egholm was still talking about the manifold vicissitudes of his life.

He had started as a grocer's assistant in Helsingør, then in Aalborg; after that he had been a photographer, in the time of the war, when the Austrians were there. He had made a fortune, but it had vanished in an attempt to double it, in Göteborg, Sweden, where there was no photographer at that time at all. Then on to Copenhagen with but a few small coins remaining, and, despite this adverse beginning, the possession of the biggest photographic studio in the town a few months later.

This was Egholm's *chef-d'œuvre*; he had told the story of it a hundred times. And by frequent repetition, it had gained a certain style, as he omitted more and more of the commonplace. He told of his bold advertisements—a new departure altogether—his growing staff of assistants, the eagerness of the public to come first, and the tearful envy of his competitors. And when, in the flight of his telling, he reached its highest point, where he really was the greatest photographer in the place—he stopped. He felt he must remain there on those heights, above the clouds; he wished his hearers always to remember him as there and so. The miserable descent he passed over, and began as a matter of course with his appointment on the railways, as station assistant, at a wretched rate of pay.

Vang did not seem to miss the intervening chapters; he sat wallowing in the delicious smell of cooking that came through from the kitchen.

Egholm told of his railway period, how he had rushed about the country, now at some desolate little station on the Jutland moors, now in big places like Odense or Frederikshavn. He sighed, and passed over the conflicts with authority, and his dismissal. No, he would not think of those things now; not a thought. He turned abruptly to the annals of the Brethren of St. John. True, there was much that was disappointing about his relations with that community, but, after all, there had been something grand in its way about the final meeting. Had he not stood there alone, and told them the truth, in such a wise that even the fellow from Copenhagen had polished his glasses and shaken in his shoes, finding nothing to say in return? Had he not gained the victory? They had thrown him out—but was not that in itself sufficient evidence that his words were true, and had pierced them accordingly?

"Yes, and then I heard a shout from someone down by the door; it was Meilby. You know, the photographer I used to teach English. He was rather like you, by the way, Vang—the same gentle sort of eyes...."

Augh! Egholm realised suddenly that he had said that once before to-day. He had got to the end of his repertoire. A sense of shame came over him, he cleared his throat, and cried in a forced voice:

"Hi, Anna! Vang says he'll have his money back if the performance doesn't begin very soon."

Vang grunted; that was the sort of thing he understood. But Fru Egholm shivered in fear.

"Yes, yes, in a minute—five minutes more! Hedvig, for Heaven's sake, look and see if it's nearly done?"

"Yes; it's peeling now," reported Hedvig, and her mother left the horseradish to go and taste the soup. *Herregud!* it was as weak as ditchwater. She closed her eyes, and tasted once again, looking very much like a blinking hen herself. "Ditchwater, simply!"

"Hedvig!" She routed out a pocket-handkerchief, and untied a twenty-five *øre* from one corner. "Run out and get a quarter of butter, there's a dear."

"Well, and what then?" she said sullenly to herself. "It's got to be used, and I'm not sorry I did it. Egholm always likes his things a little on the rich side, and now after he's been so angry...."

It was hard to please him anyway when he was in that mood. Who would have thought he could have turned so furious just for a little remark like that? ... What was it now she had happened to say?

Her brain was puzzling to remember it as she bustled about the final preparations. She talked to herself in an undertone, weeping silently the while.

"Anna, what do you think you're doing out there?" cried Egholm.

Hedvig answered with a brief, sharp word, which her mother tried to cover with a "Sh!"

"Yes, dear—yes," she called.

At the last moment she had hit upon a new and ingenious plan for saving her housewifely credit. The soup could be served up in the plates outside, and brought to table thus; the nasty dish thing could be used for the fowl itself. Fortunately, Vang might not know it was a developing tank at all.

Hedvig carried Vang's plate in, walking stiffly as a wooden doll, and biting her lips till they showed white. But Vang, with a single friendly tug at her pigtails, made her open her mouth at once.

She laughed, showing her fresh white teeth. That was Hedvig's way.

Vang gulped down the hot soup with a gurgling noise like a malstrøm. Egholm looked across nervously and enviously, and when Hedvig came round behind his chair, he reached out backwards greedily, but was sadly disappointed. No second helping—only the big geranium that Hedvig had brought in to set in the middle of the table. This was her mother's last brilliant effort; no one could see now that the plates were not alike. She had even fastened paper round the pot, as if it were a birthday tribute.

They ate in silence, but when the dish was empty, and each was wrenching at his skinny, fleshless wing, Vang let off his long-restrained witticism:

"Egholm, what do you say? Can a chicken swim?"

"Swim? A chicken? Why, I suppose so—no, that is, I don't think so."

"Well, shall we try if we can teach it?"

"I—I don't quite follow…. And, anyhow there's only the ghost of it left now, ha ha!"

"Well, there's time yet, for it's fluttering about just now in this little round pond just here!" Vang rose heavily, as if from repletion, snorting with delight at the success of his little joke, and drew a circle with one finger over the front of his well-expanded waistcoat. "All we want's a drop of something for it to practise in!"

Hedvig was dispatched to buy *akvavit* with the few coins Vang found in his pockets; he gave her the most precise instructions as to which particular brand it was to be.

Egholm never drank with his meals as a rule, but that evening he took three glasses of the spirit, though it burned his throat like fire. Vang made no attempt to force him, but simply said "*Skaal!*" and tossed off his glass.

Egholm, however, had other reasons.

He had fancied he could *eat* himself into oblivion, and was trying now—with just as little effect—to drink his trouble away. But it only grew the worse.

It was Anna's eyes that would keep rising up before him.

Anna's grey-green eyes, with their frightened look, in a setting of swollen, blue, and bloodshot flesh, that hung in pouches down on either side of her nose.

It was not that he felt remorse for what he had done; that did not cost him a thought. But the effects of it—those *eyes*—haunted him now, following him everywhere he turned, relentlessly, cruelly. He writhed, and sighed, overflowing with self-pity for his troubles.

Eating did not help him, drinking was equally futile; there was but one thing to do, then—to start talking again, before it grew worse. It was nothing to what it might be yet. And Egholm launched out into a sea of talk, diving into it, swimming out into it, hoping to leave the thing that followed him outdistanced on the shore.

"And the money I made in Aalborg when the Austrians were there—you've no idea. My studio was simply besieged by all those black-bearded soldiers with their strings and stripes—and they'd no lack of cash, I can tell you. But then while they were sitting about waiting, there would come some slip of a lieutenant and turn the whole lot of them out to make way for him. And one dirty thief I remember that wouldn't pay—between you and me, the photos were not much good, and that's the truth. Showed him with three or four heads, you understand. But the General simply told him to pay up sharp, if he didn't want his brains blown out. And that settled it. The General, of course, was a particular friend of mine. I'll tell you while I think of it. It was this way. He wanted his photo taken, of course, like all the rest of them, but he must have it done up at the castle itself, in the great hall, and that was as dark as a cellar. I managed to get him out on the steps at last, though he cursed and swore all the time, and hacked about on the stone paving with his spurs. All the others got out of the way—sloped off like shadows—and there was I all alone with him, in a ghastly fright, and making a fearful mess of things with the camera. The interpreter had vanished, too. Then, just as I was ready, at the critical moment, you understand, I rapped out in German, 'Now! Look pleasant, please!' All photographers used to do that, you know, in those days. I said it without thinking.

"You should have seen him. First he swore like the very devil; you could almost see the blue flames dancing round him. But then he burst out laughing.

"He wanted me to go back to Austria with him. Tried all he knew to get me to go."

Egholm sighed, and gazed vacantly before him, trying if the vision that haunted him were gone.

... Eyes, eyes. Eyes full of terror, set in patches of bruised flesh, and a drop of congealed blood just at the side of the nose....

He sprang violently to his feet, and started talking about Göteborg. The canals, where the women did their washing, the park, Trädgården, and Masthugget, where he had been out one Sunday. He talked Swedish, and gave a long account of a funeral—Anna had lost one child in Göteborg—the first.

Meanwhile, Vang was quietly getting to the bottom of the bottle, and when at last Egholm, weary of his desperate fluttering on empty words, flung himself down, Vang felt that it was *his* turn to speak.

"Ahem!—seeing no other gentleman has risen Henrik Vang now begs to propose: 'The Ladies.' My friend, my old and faithful friend, wake up and listen to my words. You have honoured me. You have invited me to share your board. The supper was good—rather tough, that fowl, but, after all, that's neither here nor there. In a word, you have done me a great honour, and I propose then to honour you in return. My friend, my old and faithful friend, you are a *man*. You can assert yourself, and get your own way. But Henrik Vang, he can't. And I ask you now: How shall we gain the mastery over woman? There! That, my friend, is the problem—the problem of the future."

"But is it true that she knocks you about?" asked Egholm, grasping eagerly at anything to turn the current of his own thoughts.

"Sh! Wait. Let me. I'll tell you the whole story, from the time when she was parlourmaid at the house. I was only a boy, really—it was just after Mother had died. No—I won't begin there, though. Nothing happened, really, till four or five years after, when I came home after I'd been out in the world a bit. Therese had got to be housekeeper, then. And Father, he said I was to leave her alone. Well, that of course put me on to her at once. There were enough of them about I could have got if I'd cared—what do you think? Ah, you don't know the sort of man Henrik Vang was to look at in those days! But she was nearest to hand, of course. Ever so near.... Oh! And handsome, that she was. In two layers, as you might say, one outside the other. Father, he was after us whenever he got a chance. He offered me his gold watch to leave her alone, but I wasn't such a fool. I'd have that anyway when he was gone, and I told him so. But then one day comes Therese and shows me where he'd been pinching her—arms black and blue. Well, I wasn't going to stand that, you know, so we got a special licence, and went off and got married in Fredericia. Father, he didn't know about it, of course, and when he sees us coming up the steps arm in arm, he says: 'Henrik, do you know I've kept that girl ever since your mother died?' 'That's as may be,' says I. 'Anyhow, she's mine now.' And then I up and showed him our wedding ring—cost me ten *kroner*, it did. Then says he: 'Out you get—out of my house. A thousand *kroner* a year, that's all you'll get. The hotel here I'll keep, as long as I've strength to lift a glass!'"

The tears flowed down over Vang's puffy purple cheeks. Egholm sniffed once or twice in sympathy, and forgot his own troubles for a moment.

Vang licked a last drop from the neck of the bottle, and went on:

"Well, you see, Therese had never expected that—nor had I. But don't let's talk about me. What *was* I to expect? Drunken fool, that's all. Perhaps it was that made her turn religious. I don't know. I never can think things out. It tires me. Well, she said to me: 'Look here, you get me a place at the Postmaster's or the Stationmaster's, or one of those you're always drinking with.' Well, they simply laughed at me. But the religious lot, they didn't mind. Only the worst of it was, from the time she set her thoughts on heaven, it's been simply hell for me! Now, how d'you explain that?"

Egholm saw him off, going out to the gate with him, and at the same moment Hedvig opened the kitchen door. Yes, the dish was empty. A good thing they had helped themselves before it went in.

They lit the lamp, and began making things ready for the night. There was a jumble of things in every corner. Empty bottles by the dozen, and in one place she found a parcel, carefully wrapped in newspaper, containing the skins and skeleton remains of smoked herrings. Father, no doubt, thought that was the easiest way of clearing up after him.

"We'll sleep in the little room, of course," said Hedvig firmly to her mother.

"Ye—es," said her mother quietly. But as Hedvig began dragging the bedding across, she put on her sternest face, and said:

"Never you mind where your mother's to sleep or not to sleep. You know your Bible, don't you, enough to remember about man and wife being one?"

"Ho!"

"But I'll be there under the window. Yes, that's best."

"I know what I'd have done if I'd been you," said Hedvig firmly. "I wouldn't have washed that dish."

"The one with the poison! Heavens, child—why, they might have been ever so ill!"

"*They might have died!*" Hedvig's eyes were almost white to look at as she spoke.

At the same moment Egholm came in again, and now nothing was heard but the rattle of the iron bedsteads and flapping of sheets and bedclothes patted down. They shared for better or worse. Hedvig was given one iron bedstead in the little room to herself, but had to be content with a woollen blanket and her father's old railway cloak for covering. Fru Egholm had to spread her mattress on the floor till they could get the settee screwed together; then she had a real down coverlet over.

Egholm began undressing without a word. His wife turned down the lamp—there were no curtains to the windows. They heard him drop his waistcoat over by the coal-scuttle, and his trousers by the door; then he threw himself on his bed, breathing heavily.

Fru Egholm stole into the little room, where Emanuel's cradle was set against Hedvig's bed, lest the master of the house should be disturbed.

Sleeping soundly, the little angel.

"Hedvig dear, you've kept your stockings on, haven't you?"

"Oh, I'm warm enough—just feel here." She found her mother's hand and drew it down over some thick woollen stuff, that felt strange to the fingers.

"What—what is it?"

"Look and see!"

Fru Egholm closed the door and struck a match. There lay Hedvig, covered over with a curious black rug with a silver fringe round the edges and a cross in the centre.

For a moment she was dazed, then, calling up some distant memory, she exclaimed in horror:

"Heavens, child! Why, it's the pall they use for the hearse! Wherever did you get it?"

"It was hanging on the stairs outside," said Hedvig, with a grin.

"But you mustn't. However could you, Hedvig! That you could ever dare.... Come! We must put it back at once."

Hedvig made as if to obey, and drew the thing down, but the moment her legs were free, she turned a back-somersault and commenced a wild topsy-turvy dance in the air, waving her feet about like a catherine-wheel. Then suddenly she disappeared again under the pall, showing not so much as the tip of her nose.

The match went out. Fru Egholm shook her head anxiously, with a faint smile, and stole out of the room. Hedvig—what a child!

All was quiet in the parlour now. Egholm was apparently asleep. Pray God he might wake in a better mood!

Anyhow, they had got that fellow Vang out of the house at last—and if she could manage it, he should not be in a hurry to come again. He'd a bad influence. The way he spoke about his wife—Egholm would never have talked like that himself! A nice sort of fellow, indeed—and his father owned a hotel!

Her breast heaved as she undressed and laid her things neatly on a chair, as her father had taught her when a child. She listened breathlessly—was Egholm asleep?

Should she?... He didn't deserve it—but why think of that now?

Softly she dragged the mattress from under the window, a little way over the floor, stopped, listened, and dragged it a little farther. Then she started at a sound, and felt ashamed, as if she had been a thief trying to steal her own bed.

Little by little she edged her way along, and finally crept under the clothes with a sigh of resignation.

When he awoke, he should find her humble couch on the floor beside his bed.

XII

But Egholm was not asleep; only lying quite still, with wide-open eyes.

His trouble was that going to bed only made him wakeful, however sleepy he might have been while undressing. It generally took him a couple of hours to get to sleep, and during that time his eyes seemed to acquire a power of inward vision. The experiences of the day lifted their coffin lid and swarmed out from his brain-cells as terrifying apparitions in the dark.

True, it might happen at times, as now to-day, that they also appeared in the daytime, but then he could ward them off as long as he kept on talking and talking incessantly.

But at night! They laughed at him in horrid wise, lifted the wrappings from their skulls, and blinked at him with empty eye-sockets. He was *theirs*.

Nevertheless, he had developed a certain method in his madness; they could not take him by surprise now, as they had done at first.

To-day, he had struck Anna three times in the face—no light blows either, for he could feel his knuckles slightly tender still—well and good, then to-night the result would be that he found Anna exchanged for Clara Steen, the child with the deep eyes, the splendid Clara of youth, the beloved little maiden in the gold frame.

In a gold frame—yes, an oval gold frame.

Here again was one of those ridiculous things that could, given the opportunity and a suitable mood, make a man laugh himself crooked.

Egholm turned over on the other side, and set himself to think through the whole affair from the beginning, how it had started when he had first gone as a boy to work in Konsul Steen's business in Helsingør.

The memory here was sweet as a breath from gardens of lilac, and was intended solely to form a nice, crude background of contrast to that which was to come. Yes, Egholm knew the system of these things.

He saw himself as a slender, brown-eyed, curly-haired lad running about upstairs and down in the big store, hauling at casks and pulling out drawers, followed everywhere by the sharp eyes of Jespersen, the assistant.

Now down into the cellar for rum, now to the warehouse for dried fish, then up to the huge loft for tobacco. Up there was the place he liked best; not only were the finest goods kept there, breathing essences of the whole world towards him from cases of spice, but he loved the view from the slip-door, out over the Sound and the fortress of Kronborg, and the red roofs of the town.

From north and south came ships with proudly upright masts and rigging, heaving to while the Customs officers went on board. And each of them utilised the opportunity to lay in provisions. Kasper Egholm was rowed out to them with heavy boat-loads of wares, and was soon at home on vessels of all nations—Dutch, English, French, and Russian. He even began to feel himself familiar with the languages.

It was from here he had first caught sight of Clara, Konsul Steen's daughter.

Possibly it was as much for her sake as for anything else that he loved to throw open the slip-door, or climb up to a window in the roof.

One little episode he remembered as distinctly as if it had happened yesterday.

He had been set to counting Swedish nails, a hundred to each packet, but, seeing his chance, used the scales instead. It was ever so much easier to weigh them out, than with all that everlasting counting; also, he could finish in no time, and be free to loiter by the window and dream.

The wind blows freshly about his ears, he looks over toward the grey-green slopes of the Swedish coast, and feels himself as free as if his glance could carry him over the Sound, high over the roofs, and green trees, and the top-masts of the ships.

Suddenly he cranes his neck forward, and a flood of warmth surges from his heart to his cheeks, swelling the veins of his neck; *there*, on the gravel path just below, in his master's garden, walks Clara.

White stockings and little low shoes; her footsteps shoot forward like the narrow-leaved bine of some swiftly growing plant, and she hums in time to her walk. Kasper is so fascinated that involuntarily he hums as well, but wakes with a start of fright at hearing his own rough voice. He fancies he can see the delicate skin of her neck gleaming through the lace edge of her dress, the blue pulse in her temples, and the play of the sunlight in her dark-brown hair.

She walks round the lawn, and turns into a patch that would take her along under the wall, where Kasper cannot follow. He realises this, and works his way right out on to the roof, with only his legs dangling down inside.

"Clara, dear little Jomfru Clara," whispers his mouth, "do not go away!"

At the same moment his legs are gripped by powerful claws, and he is hauled down with such force and suddenness that he has not time even to put out his hands. Down he comes anyhow on the floor, and lies there, bruised and shaken, looking up into Jespersen's green eyes.

"Ho! So you loaf about looking out of the window when you ought to be counting nails!"

And now it was discovered that he had used the scales. Jespersen found one packet with ninety-eight nails and another with a hundred and one instead of a hundred, and ran off to tell his master. Next day Kasper was sent for from the inner office.

The thought of this is a culmination of delight for Egholm in his sleepless state, but at the same time, he notes, in parenthesis, as it were, that he is now on the brink of the abyss he *knows* will shortly swallow him up.

The stately man with the dark, full beard talks to him of doing one's duty to the utmost, not merely as far as may be seen. And during the speech Kasper discovers on the leather-covered wall a picture in a gilded oval frame—a painting of Clara.

To him it seems even more lovely, even more living, than the girl herself; his eyes are simply held spellbound to the beautiful vision.

Konsul Steen glances absently in the same direction, and then, with a very eloquent gesture, places himself between Kasper and his daughter.

"Have you already forgotten your duties in life, which your parents, honest people, I have no doubt, taught you? What did you say your father was?"

"I'm a foundling," says the boy, with dignity, enjoying his master's embarrassment.

Afterwards, standing out in the passage, he remembers only that one question and answer. But, most of all, Clara's portrait is burned deep into his brain. Many a time he steals a peep at it through the keyhole. Even in the golden days when Clara's living self would place her hand in his and follow him adventuring through the gloomy cellars, or over mountains of sacks to the topmost opening of the loft, telling him her troubles and her joys, and listening to all *his* confessions, with her firm, commanding, and yet so innocent eyes fixed on his—even then the painting did not lose its halo. And throughout the many years of struggle, it lived on in his joy and his anguish, mostly in anguish, it is true, for there was certainly nothing merely amusing when it rose up like life before his mental vision, in all its smiling, merciless beauty, rendering his agony tenfold worse. Egholm had spoken to several people about that same thing, among them the doctor at the hospital where he had once been a patient for some time. The doctor knew that sort of thing very well; it was what was called an *obsession*. Well and good—but was that any explanation, after all? No; it was rather something mysterious, something of the nature of magic, that had come into his life from the time he married Anna.

Anna—yes....

He writhed and twisted in his bed, as if he were on a spit. His heart pumped audibly and irregularly.

To begin with, she had opened the door, letting out all the warmth, and made him nervous with all the things she strewed about the floor.

Then there had been that trouble about the dark-room, which had driven him out of his senses with its insistence.

Why couldn't she understand that it was not her his blows were aimed at, but at Fate?

What was a photographer without a dark-room?

No—she could not understand. Not an atom. She could only stand there and say "But, Egholm...." and plague him about her kitchen.

Egholm half raised himself in bed, utterly in the power of his nightmare thoughts, and struck wildly at the air with his clenched fist.

The vision—yes, there it was!

"*Herregud!*—can't a man be left to sleep in peace?" he murmured offendedly, yet with a sort of humility at the same time. "I'm so tired...."

But as in the gleam of lightning he saw again and again Jomfru Clara, and at last she stood there clearly, steadfastly, with her great deep and mischievous eyes radiantly upon him.

He groaned and shuddered, flinging himself desperately about as he lay, for he knew what was coming now.

Hastily, mechanically, he ran through the scene once more. There stood Anna, and there he himself....

"But, Egholm...."

"You are the serpent...."

His fist shot out into the dark, and struck, this time, not Anna, but the pale, bright girl who seemed to glide into her place.

"Oh—oh!" He writhed and groaned again, drawing in his breath between closed lips, as one who has suddenly cut a deep wound in his hand.

"Aren't you well, dear?" It was Anna's voice, close at hand.

He lay stiff and still, hardly breathing now. The interruption had driven the horrors away.

Ridiculous—but so it was with him. He remembered, for instance, having been haunted by a snake—one he had seen preserved in spirits at some railway station office or other ... yes. That had stopped, after a while, of itself. But it was worse with Clara's picture. In a way, it was more beautiful, of course—oh, so beautiful....

He yawned audibly.

But he thought many other things out yet: of his business and his money affairs; of Vang and Vang's domestic life; of an invention he wanted to get on with—a thing of almost world-revolutionary importance, a steam turbine, that could go forward or back like lightning. It would make him a rich man—a wealthy man....

A little later he dropped off to sleep, lying on his back, and breathing still in little unsteady gasps.

Fru Egholm's straw mattress creaked as she rose quietly, and with a gentle touch here and there tucked his bedclothes close about him.

In the next room Hedvig was talking in her sleep—something about cakes....

"*Herregud!*" murmured her mother—"dreaming of cakes means illness. I hope it doesn't mean Emanuel's going to get the chickenpox."

With a sigh she fell off to sleep.

The clock struck two.

XIII

Madam Hermansen came into every house in Knarreby, without exception—whence follows, that she came to Egholm's.

How she managed to effect an entry there, where shutters and bolts were carefully set to hide the shame of poverty, is not stated.

Presumably, she came of herself, like most diseases—and she came again and again, like a series of bad relapses. She literally clung to the Egholms, and almost neglected her other visits therefor.

They were somehow more remarkable than others, she thought. They had a past.

Madam Hermansen herself was tolerated—almost, one might say, esteemed. At any rate, no attempt was ever made to find a cure for her. Egholm enjoyed the abundant laughter with which she greeted even the most diluted sample of his wit, and Fru Egholm needed someone to *confide in*.

It was all very well for *him*. In his all too extensive leisure, he made excursions through the town, spending hours in talk with fishermen down at the harbour, or going off for solitary walks along the shore or in the woods. *She*, on the other hand, could only trip about in the two small rooms, with never a sight of the sun beyond the narrow strip that drew like the hand of a clock across the kitchen floor from four till half-past seven in the morning. And no one to talk to but her husband and the children. Little wonder, then, that the flow of speech so long held back poured forth in flood when Madam Hermansen began deftly working at the sluices.

The talk itself was but a detail, that cropped up before one knew, thought Fru Egholm at times; but if she had not had someone to look at her needlework, why, in the long run, it would mean sinking down to the level of a man.

True, Madam Hermansen was no connoisseur of art, but a dollymop who never achieved more than the knitting of stockings herself. On the other hand, she was ready to prostrate herself in admiration of even the most trivial piece of embroidery or crochet-work. There was something in that....

"Why, it almost turns my head only to look at it," she declared, fingering the coverlet for the chest of drawers. It was one afternoon in May, and the two women were alone in the house with little Emanuel.

"Oh, you could learn it yourself in five minutes." Fru Egholm flushed with pride, and her hands flew over the work. "No, but you should see a thing I made just before we left Odense. Fancy crochet."

"Heaven preserve us! Me! Never to my dying day! It's more than I'm ever likely to learn, I'm sure. What was it you called it?"

"Fancy crochet. And then I lost it—it was a cruel shame, really. And such a lovely pattern."

"Stolen?" cried Fru Hermansen, slapping her thighs.

"No. I gave it away to a woman that came up to congratulate when Emanuel was born. She praised it up, and I saw what she meant, of course. But here's another thing you must see."

She rose, and took out a pin-cushion from a drawer.

"There's nothing special about that, of course...."

But Madam Hermansen declared she had never seen anything like it. The pale pink silk showing all glossy through under the crochet cover was simply luxurious.

"Ah yes! That's the sort of things a body would like to have about the house," she said, turning it over in her chapped and knotty hands. "And what do you use a thing like that for, now?"

"Oh, fine ladies use it for brooches and things. But it's mostly meant for a young girl, you know, to have on a chest of drawers, this way...."

"Yes, yes, that's much the best. Why, it would be a sin and a shame to stick pins in a thing like that."

"Look here," said Fru Egholm, flushing, "you keep it. Yes, do; it's yours. No, no; do as I say—and we'll speak no more about it."

Madam Hermansen made a great fuss of protest, but allowed herself to be persuaded, and thrust it under her shawl. She held it as if it had been a live lobster.

And Fru Egholm brought out other things. There was a newspaper holder worked with poppies, and a cushion embroidered on canvas.

"There's little pleasure in having them," she sighed. "Egholm, he doesn't value it more than the dirt under his feet."

"Ah! It's just the same with Hermansen, now. One Sunday afternoon I came home and found him, as true as I'm here, sitting on the curtains, smoking, as careless as could be. But your husband—I thought he was a model."

"Egholm doesn't smoke. If he did, he'd be just the same. But I can tell you a thing—just to show what he thinks about my work. Ah, Madam Hermansen, take my word for it, there's many a slight a woman has to put up with that hurts more than all your blows."

"And he's been on the railway, too...."

"It doesn't change human nature, after all. It was these here things from the auction at Gammelhauge, the mirror and the chest of drawers, and the big chair over by the window, and that very one you're sitting in now. Now, tell me honestly, would you call them nice to look at?"

Madam Hermansen shifted a little under in her big green shawl.

"They're a trifle old fashioned to my mind." And she sniffed disdainfully.

"Old fashioned and worm eaten and heavy and clumsy—you needn't be afraid to say it. Why, it's almost two men's work to lift a chair like that. And as for the glass—why, it makes you look like a chimney-sweep. The chest of drawers is not so bad; it does hold a good deal. Wools and odds and ends.... But, all the same...."

"My daughter she had one with nickel handles to pull out," said Madam Hermansen, poking at it. "And walnut's the nicest you can have, so the joiner man said."

"Yes, that's what I say. But what do you think Egholm said? 'Rare specimens,' he said—'solid mahogany!' Ugh! Well, do you know what I did? I set to work then and there and made up something to cover the worst of it. Those butterflies for the rocking-chair, and the cloth with the stars on for the chest of drawers, and paper roses to put in by the mirror. It took me the whole of a night, but I wouldn't have grudged it, if I'd only got a thimbleful of thanks for my pains. And now, just listen, and I'll tell you the thanks I got. One day the Sanitary Inspector came round to have a look at the sink. He'd brought a whole crowd with him—it was a commission or something, with the mayor and the doctor and the vet, and so on. Then one of them gets it into his head he'd like to have a look round the place. Egholm, of course, waves his hand and says, 'With pleasure.' And never a thought in his head of anything the matter."

Madam Hermansen nodded sympathetically.

"Well, they came in through the kitchen and stood there poking about at the sink for a bit, and while they're at it, Egholm comes in here. And then—what do you say to this?—he rushes round the room and pulls it all off. As true as I'm here; the butterflies and the paper flowers, and the toilet cover and all. Threw the flowers under the table, and stuffed the rest in under his coat. Now, if that isn't simply disgraceful...."

"And what did you *say* to him?" Madam Hermansen shook herself, giving out a perfume of leeks and celery from under her shawl.

"Not a word. I had to keep it all back, and bow and scrape to the gentlemen, with my heart like to bursting all the time. 'We must take all that stuff out of the way when anyone comes,' he says after. Oh, he's that full of his fashionable notions, there's no room for human feeling in his breast. And if there is one thing I can't abide, it is that fashionable nonsense."

"Well, now, I don't know that it's altogether put on, you know, with him, seeing he's a man of good family, as you might say."

"Good family—h'm. As to that...." Fru Egholm raised her eyebrows.

"Well, well, I don't know, of course," said Madam Hermansen, shifting heavily a little forward. "I thought he was a parson's son, and his parents were dead?"

"No, indeed he's not. Nothing of the kind."

"He's not a circus child, is he?—there's some say he is."

"It wouldn't be so surprising, with all his antics generally. But the real truth is, he's a foundling—that is to say, illegitimate." Fru Egholm uttered the last word with a certain coldness, but a moment after sighed compassionately.

"You don't say so! Well, now, I never did...." Madam Hermansen sat rocking backwards and forwards in ecstasy, and as she realised what a grand piece of news she had got hold of, a silent laughter began bubbling up from her heart.

Fru Egholm looked at her in some surprise, and, uncertain how to take her, bent over the cradle and busied herself with the child.

"Why, then, Madam Danielsen was right, after all," said Madam Hermansen. "But who was his mother, then?"

"Well, to tell the truth, she was a fine lady, and married a professor after—and that's a strange thing, seeing what a plenty of honest girls there are about. She must have been a baggage, though, all the same, to get into trouble like that."

"Yes, indeed," said Madam Hermansen, patting the hairpins that jostled each other in a knot of hair about the size of a walnut. "And his father?"

"Oh, a scatter-brained fellow. Government official, they called him, but he was a painter—an artist, you know—besides, and I daresay it was that was his undoing in the end, when he led the girl astray."

"But I thought the doctors at the Foundling Hospital were under oath not to tell who the parents were?"

"That's true enough. But d'you think Egholm would be put off like that? No, he set to work—that is, when he was grown up—and advertised in *Berlingske Tidende*, putting it all in, so-and-so, as if he didn't know what shame was. And then his sister—half-sister, that is, of course—wrote and came along of her own accord. Nice enough in her way, she was, too, but you could see she was one of the same sort...."

Fru Egholm made a grimace involving numerous wrinkles of the nose. Madam Hermansen nodded as one who understood.

"Yes ... she gave herself out for an artist, like her father had been—and she was the image of him to look at, too."

"But I thought...."

"Well, that of course, in a way. For they said she used to go sitting in a public place and painting pictures with a man stark naked as a model."

"Heaven preserve us!" gasped Madam Hermansen. "In all my born days.... Well, she must have been a nice one."

"She and Egholm simply slobbered over each other with their affected ways. She called him her dear lost brother, and how glad she was to find him again—and all that sort of thing. I simply said there was no need to carry on too much about it that I could see, for if they had grown up together, like as not they'd have been tearing each other's eyes out. He was a terrible child, I believe—used to pour sand over the cake-man's basket outside Rundetaarn, and let off fireworks in the street and so on."

"And his father wouldn't acknowledge him, then?"

"No. That is to say, his father made haste and died when the boy was only four or five about, but he'd had the grace to set aside a little money beforehand, so Egholm could have the most expensive schooling there ever was. And it's left its pretty mark on him, as you can hear when he speaks."

"Well, in the way of politeness, as you might say, he certainly is," said Fru Hermansen warmly.

"Puh! When there's anyone about, yes," said Fru Egholm. She was not in the humour for praising her husband just now. "But what's he like at home? Ah—that's where you get to know people's hearts!"

And before she knew it, she had lifted the roof off their entire abode, making plain to her visitor that which had formerly been shrouded in darkness.

It was not a little.

Madam Hermansen was simply speechless when Fru Egholm showed her, with tears, the scars under her eyes and the little spot by the temple where the hair was gone.

"I can't understand you staying another day," she said, when the sufferer stuck fast in a sob.

"Oh, you mustn't talk like that. When you've vowed before the altar...."

"Did *he* vow before the altar to knock you about like that, eh? Did he say anything about that?"

"No—o." Fru Egholm laughed through her tears, anxious to bring her visitor to a gentler frame of mind. "No, and it would be no more than his deserts if I said I wouldn't live with him any more. But I can't help it; it's not in my nature to do it. And, after all, it's his business how he treats his wife, isn't it? What's it to do with me? I couldn't think of living anywhere but where he is. Love's not a thing you can pull up by the roots all of a sudden.

> "'When first the flame of love warms human heart, they little know
> What harm they do beyond repair who make it cease to glow!'"

"Hymns!" said Madam Hermansen scornfully.

"Ah, but it's just hymns and such that lift us up nearer to God."

"Oh, God's all right, of course, but it doesn't do in this world to leave too much to God."

"It's all we poor sinful mortals have. Where do you suppose I should ever find comfort and solace if I hadn't God to turn to? Why, He's almighty. He's even done things with Egholm at times. When I think of it, I feel ashamed of myself that I ever can sit and complain. Now, just by way of example.... It was the day we came over here from Odense, me and the children. I'd no sooner got out of the train than he puts his arms round me and kisses me right on the cheek. And what's the most marvellous thing about it all—I can't understand it to this day—he did it right in front of three or four girls standing staring at us all the time. Ah, Madam Hermansen, take my word for it, a little thing like that gives you strength to live on for a long time after. And then Egholm's been good to me in other ways. He knows—Lord forgive me that I should say it—that I'm more of a God-fearing sort than he is himself. And—I don't know how to put it—that my God's—well, more genuine, as you might say, than his. I'll tell you how I found that out, Madam Hermansen. You know it was said the end of the world was to come a few years back. It was in all the papers, and Egholm, he took it all in for gospel truth, because he said it agreed with the signs in the Revelations, you know...."

"And did it come?"

"Why, of course it didn't—or we shouldn't be sitting here now, should we? But Egholm, he was as sure as could be it was going to happen, on the thirteenth of November, and when it was only the eighth, he came and told me to make up a bed for one of us on the floor. We'd always been used to sleep together in one bed."

"But what did he want to change for?" asked Madam Hermansen, with increasing interest.

"Why," explained Fru Egholm eagerly, "you see—he confessed himself why it was; he was wonderfully gentle those days. He wouldn't have us sleeping together—not because of anything indecent or that sort, but because it says in the Bible that on the Day of Judgment there may be two people sleeping in the same bed, 'and the one shall be taken and the other left.'"

"So, you see. Madam Hermansen, I soon reckoned out what he thought, how I might get to heaven after all."

"And he's never been in love with anybody—*outside*, I mean?"

"There's one he's in love with," laughed Fru Egholm—"more than anything else in the world. And that's—himself! No, thank goodness he's never had time for that sort of thing, being too busy with his steam-engine inventions. Now I think of it, though, there was a girl once, when he was quite young, over in Helsingør. Clara Steen was her name. You'll have heard of Consul Steen, no doubt; he's ever so rich. His daughter, it was. And she ran after him to such a degree.... Why, he used to write verses to her. Though I don't count that anything very much against him, for he's written poetry to me, too, in the days when we were engaged."

She thrust a practised hand into her workbox, and fished up a yellowed scrap of paper, and read:

> "'Helsingør by waters bright
> Like a Venice to the sight,
> All the world thy fame doth know.
> Beeches fair around thee grow,
> And the fortress with its crown

Looks majestically down,...'"

Fru Hermansen relapsed into an envious silence, absently investigating her nostrils with one finger. Fru Egholm took out some new hair, and compared the colour with that she was using.

"Think that will do?" she asked ingratiatingly.

"Well, it ought to. It's a deal prettier than the other."

"But it oughtn't to be! You're supposed to have all the same coloured hair in one plait."

"Ugh! I've no patience with all their affected ways," said Fru Hermansen sullenly. She was disappointed at finding the conversation turned to something of so little interest by comparison. "What was I going to say now?" she went on. "Was it just lately he knocked you about like that?"

"Ye—es, of course. But no worse than before. Not nearly so bad. And anyhow, if he did, I suppose it was God's will. Or else, perhaps, he can't help it, by reason of always having an unruly mind."

She checked herself with a sudden start, and her busy hands fell to patting aimlessly here and there.

"I think it must be toothache," she said in a loud, drawling, careless voice, altogether different from her former manner.

"Toothache?..." Madam Hermansen sat with her mouth wide open for a moment—then she, too, caught the sound of Egholm's approaching step. "Yes, yes, of course, it would be toothache, yes, yes...." And she chuckled with a sound like the rattle of a rake on a watering-can.

"Emanuel, I mean, of course," said Fru Egholm confusedly, as her husband walked in. He was carrying a huge paper bag, that looked as if it might burst at any minute.

He set it down carefully, and joined in the conversation.

"Now, if only Anna would let me," he said eagerly, "I'd cure that child in no time."

"I've heard you can do all sorts of wonders, so people say." Fru Hermansen leaned back with her hands folded across her lap, and looked up admiringly at Egholm.

"Why, I know a trifle of the secrets of Nature, that's all. As for toothache, there's no such thing. The youngster there—what's his name, now? —Emanuel, is suffering from indigestion, nothing more. Give him a plate of carrots chopped up fine, mixed with equal parts of sand and gravel, morning and evening, and he'd be all right in a couple of days."

"Never as long as I live!" said Fru Egholm.

"Powdered glass is very effective, too," went on Egholm, encouraged by Fru Hermansen's laughter, and putting on a thoughtful expression.

"I'll not see a child of mine murdered that or any other way," said the mother.

"Oh, but you'd see what a difference it would make. I'm quite in earnest. Haven't you heard that fowls have to have gravel? I noticed it myself yesterday with my own eyes, saw them pecking it up. And the idea came to me at once. I've half a mind, really, to set up as a quack doctor...."

Egholm was interrupted by a sudden splash behind him. The paper bag he had placed on the chest of drawers, dissolved by the moisture of something within, had burst; a lump of squashy-looking semi-transparent stuff had slipped to the floor, and more threatened to follow.

Fru Egholm, sorrowful and indignant, hurried to save her embroidered slip from further damage.

"Don't go spoiling my jelly-fish! Better bring a plate, or a dish or something."

"What on earth are they for, now?" asked Madam Hermansen.

"That's a great secret. For the present, at any rate. Well, I don't know; I may as well tell you, perhaps. These ... are jelly-fish—Medusæ." He tipped the contents out into a washing-basin, and poked about among the quivering specimens. "Look, here's a red one—the sort they call stingers. If you touch one, it stings you like nettles. The others are harmless—just touch one and try. Smooth and luscious, like soapsuds, what?"

Madam Hermansen advanced one hand hesitatingly, but drew it back with a scream.

"Isn't it?" said Egholm, undismayed. "Well, now, what do you think they're for? Shall I tell you? Why, *soap!* There's only one thing lacking to make them into perfect soap—a touch of lime to get a grip on the dirt—and perhaps a trifle of scent. And, only think, they're lying about on the beach in thousands, all to no use. Yes ... I'll start a soap factory, that's what I'll do."

"I thought you said you were going to be a doctor," said Fru Egholm, with an innocent expression, winking at Madam Hermansen.

"Both. And then we can save on the advertising. 'Egholm's United Surgeries and Soap Factories.'"

"And one as bad as the other." Anna had to shout aloud to make herself heard through the tempest of Madam Hermansen's laughter.

"Say, rather, one as good as the other. Oh, I shall be famous all over Denmark, all over Europe. We'll have an advertisement for the doctoring on all the soap wrappers: speciality—broken legs!"

"If only you don't break your neck holding your head in the air."

"Oh, I wasn't thinking of bones," said Egholm, delighted with the effect he was producing. "I was referring to the fracture of *wooden* legs."

"Well, now, I wonder if you could set this to rights for me?" said Fru Hermansen, patting her calf.

"Easily! What's the matter?"

"Well, I don't know that it's proper for me to show you, but never mind. We're both married folk. This leg of mine's been bad for—let me see—fifteen or sixteen years it is now. And Dr. Hoff, he's no idea, the way he's messed about with it."

Fru Hermansen turned round, set her foot upon a chair, and busied herself with underclothing, tying and untying here and there, and muttering to herself the while.

"There, you have a look at it," she said at last, with a laugh, and faced round again.

She had a rag in her mouth, and her face was flushed from bending down. Her skirts were lifted to her knees.

From the ankle up over the shin, almost to the kneecap, was a long red sore, yellowish in the centre. It looked horribly like a trail of some climbing plant.

Egholm put out a hand as if to ward off the sight, and looked away. But the would-be patient said harshly:

"And you going to be a doctor! If you can't abide the smell of hot bread, then it's no good going for a baker!"

Egholm overcame his reluctance, knelt down, and began examining the leg, from the greenish-faded stocking that was gathered like an ankle-ring at the bottom, to the knee, where a garter had cut deep brownish-red furrows.

"Here's the mischief," he said, nodding wisely. "The blood can't get past here, and that's why it can't heal. You'll have to stop wearing garters at once."

"Easy to hear it's a man that's talking," laughed Fru Egholm.

"And then we must draw fresh blood to the spot. Let me see...."

"I should think you'd have seen enough by this time."

"Fresh blood...." he murmured. His mind was busy choosing and rejecting from a hundred different things; nothing seemed to satisfy him quite. A smile of irony at his own idea curved his lips; it was not such a simple matter, after all, to get to work with Egholm's United Soap Factories and Surgeries, specialising in leg troubles.

Suddenly his face brightened all over.

"Those jelly-fish—what did you do with the dish?"

"But, Egholm? what do you want them for now?"

"You leave that to me. We want something to tickle up the nerves, and draw the blood to the spot."

He picked up the "stinger"—in his coat-tails—and held it out. It was domed like a dish-cover, and ornamented with a fiery double star at the top; innumerable threads of slimy stuff hung from its lower side.

"Suppose we put that on the sore?"

Madam Hermansen, in her first amazement, had hoisted her canvas beyond all reasonable limits; now, she let all down with a run.

"None of your games with me, thank you," she said sharply.

"What?" said Egholm in surprise. "You won't? I warrant you the leg will be all in a glow in no time. And then it's a practically certain cure."

He waved the thing enticingly before her, exhibiting it from all sides, and bending it to show the venomous lips. "Why, I wouldn't mind putting it on myself."

But Madam Hermansen's face was dark and discouraging; she set about resolutely wrapping her tender spot in all its armour of rags and bandages.

"And quite right of you, I'm sure, Madam Hermansen," said Fru Egholm.

"Well, well, we must hit on something else," said Egholm. "I won't give it up. But it must be a natural cure in any case. The sources of Nature are manifold."

And by way of restoring good humour all round, he began telling the story of the furniture from Gammelhauge.

"Isn't that an elegant chair I've got there? Do for a throne; look at the coronet on the back—it's almost on my own head now as I sit here. I've just the feel of an old nobleman, a general, or a landed aristocrat, in this chair. Let's bring it up in front of the glass. What's the use of sitting on a throne with a coronet on your bald pate when you can't see yourself?"

"Now I suppose you'll be putting a new glass in the mirror—another twenty—thirty—forty—fifty *kroner* gone, but that's nothing, of course," cried Madam Hermansen.

"Not in the least, my dear lady. In *this glass* it was that the splendidly attired knights and ladies surveyed their magnificence before the feasting commenced."

It could be seen from Egholm's movements how a knight and his lady were wont to prance and preen themselves before a mirror. A little after, he added in a voice of mystery:

"I have often seen shadows moving by in there, of an evening."

"Ugh! The nasty thing! I wouldn't have it in my house for anything," said Madam Hermansen, with a shiver.

XIV

Egholm took his washing-basin across to the studio, which had been fitted up at one end of the carpenter's store shed. The jelly-fish he placed for the present as far in under the table as possible.

First of all, he must get some work done. There were Sunday's negatives to develop—he could be thinking a bit while he was doing that. Egholm found the new dark-room an excellent place for thought, free from all disturbance.

Yes, he would think over that turbine.

That jelly-fish soap business was merely an idea—quite possibly, indeed probably, a good idea. But the turbine, the *reversible steam-turbine*, was the child of his heart, born of him, conceived by him in a length of sleep-forsaken nights. Once brought forth to the world, it would be greeted with acclamation.

It was imminent, it was hovering in the air, this question of something to replace the more complicated steam-engine. The English had come very near to a solution already.

But, for all that, it might perhaps be reserved for himself, for Egholm the Dane, to show them how to make their turbine reverse.

He could think of more than one thing at a time. As long as he could cast out sufficient ballast, he could always find a new direction of the wind to carry his thought. Nearest earth was the current connected with his work, but even that was no less erratic than those of the higher strata.

Might as well try the new developer to-day, he thought to himself, and set out his dishes all ready. Then he went into the studio again, and began studying the recipes he had scrawled up from time to time on the plank wall of the dark-room. Already there were so many of them that the list reached to the floor. He had to go down on his knees to see if it said 25 gr. or 35 gr. Suddenly he forgot what he was there for, and remained lying prone, thinking only of his steam-turbine; it seemed to him the axle bearings ought to be made with a little more stability yet. The slightest oscillation, of course, would mean an escape of steam—waste of power. Then, becoming aware of his posture, he wondered how he had got there, but, finding himself on his knees, he at once, as a practical man, decided to utilise the opportunity, and started off on a long and earnest prayer to God for the furtherance of his idea. It was, indeed, not merely a point of honour with him that it should succeed, but also, he might as well confess, a hoped-for way out of his present difficulties.

The photography business had turned out a desperate failure—there was no denying it.

The only people who came at all were the peasants who came into town on Sundays. Of these, quite a good number patronised the studio, but, unfortunately, they did not always come for the photos they had ordered. They were not impressed by his skill when they found the studio situate in a woodshed at the back of Andreasen's, with the camera perched on a cement barrel instead of a tripod.

The fine folk of the place, in accordance with an established tradition, always went over to the neighbouring town for their photographs. It didn't seem to count, somehow, unless they did.

They were just as superficial in their judgment as the peasants, and paid more heed to a smart shop than to the artistic execution of the pictures.

Here Egholm laughed to himself. The photographs he turned out could hardly be included under the heading of art at all, and he knew it. But was there anything surprising in that? In the first place, how could anyone help becoming dulled by so much adversity, and in the second—oh, well, in the second place, why the devil should *he* put himself out for all and sundry, when it was only a question of time before he threw aside his mask and revealed himself as a world-renowned inventor?

Smilingly he set to rocking his plates in their bath, and as the work went on, he bored out, in his mind, the steam channels of his turbine, and decided on the cogwheel transference.

He held a negative up to the light, and recognised three of his customers grouped about the little round table. Yes, it was those three that had taken such particular care to have the labels on their beer bottles facing neatly front, towards the observer.

Ho, ho! And that was the sort one had to bow and scrape to!

Unfortunately, this business of the turbine was not a matter to be settled in a moment. Rothe, the ironfounder, had promised to make him the larger parts, and Krogh, the smith, who had at first answered gruffly and bent farther over his intricate lock work, had been completely won over as an adherent. The next thing was to procure a boat into which the turbine could be built.

Now, where on earth could he get a boat for no money at all? Well, never mind; imagine the boat was there. Then the upright boiler would have to be set in *there*, a trifle aft of midships, so that the man at the helm could stoke as well. As for the screw, that would require special treatment in these waters, where there was so much weed about. He would have to go into that.

Egholm's mind was so keen that he saw every detail. Difficulties were disposed of as fast as they appeared.

Not till the last of the plates glided into the fixing solution did he come to himself, and then to find his heart pumping like the steam-turbine at full speed. It was always like that when he had been long at work in the darkroom. He threw open the door and went out, but the light and the fresh air turned him dizzy and blind for the moment; he staggered to a bench, and had to sit there some time before he recovered.

XV

Hedvig knew how to make herself respected. She and her father glared at each other with eyes alert and claws ready, but it was rarely anything more came of it. She had a place at the baker's, running errands for six *kroner* a month, which was no small sum for a girl still at school. Anyhow, it was practically half their rent.

Yet she was a strange little creature, not like other children, and her confidence slipped somehow between her mother's fingers.

Many a night the keyhole of the door to her little room still showed a speck of light by the time the clock struck twelve, or even one. Her mother lay anxiously listening to Egholm's snore; there was no saying what terrible thing might happen if he were to wake and find it out. But Hedvig would listen to reproaches the next morning with an unfathomable expression on her face, or smile, and shake her head. The pocket of her dress bulged with a new novel every other day.

"You should tell your mother what it *says* in those silly books you're always reading," said Fru Egholm admonishingly.

"Oh, you'd never understand a word of it," was all Hedvig answered.

One day she had stuck up a picture over her bed, showing a man and a woman, tied together with a rope, flinging themselves into the water from a bridge. A yellow half-moon shone through the tree-tops and was reflected in the water. Hedvig stood quietly, apparently indifferent, as her mother tore it down and told in vehement words how sinful it was to look at such things. But when her mother moved to hold it over the lamp, the girl flung herself suddenly in front of her with wild screams, and would not be brought to her senses until she had the horrible picture safely put away in her workbox.

Now, who would ever believe that this was the same good little Hedvig that the baker's people always said a good word for, and who could always manage to find a way when it was a case of helping others! Fuel, for instance —Egholm did not seem to have the instinct of acquiring fuel. But Hedvig was a little marvel in that way—though, no doubt, it was largely through the help of Marinus in the workshop, to give him his due. He always tucked away odd bits under his work-bench for her. He was a kindly sort, was Marinus. And he seemed particularly fond of Hedvig, and she of him—that is to say, at times. For it was towards Marinus that her fickleness of humour showed itself most of all. Sometimes when she had been in the workshop she would come back and fall into a fit of miserable weeping; at other times she would rush in at once the moment he tapped with his rule on the pane, whether she wanted firewood for the kitchen or no. And as to getting any explanation out of her—that, of course, was hopeless.

Otherwise, she was particularly good at telling things, and both her father and her mother were often amused at her way of relating little things that had passed.

Her father even had a speciality of his own in this respect; he loved to hear of the money Hedvig took across the counter when she was minding shop while her mistress was at dinner.

Then it would be Wassermann, the Customs officer, who came in and bought best part of a tray of mixed pastries—he was such a sweet tooth. Then perhaps there would be a message from Etatsraadens' for sixty butter puffs for to-morrow morning.

"Sixty!" cried her father. "And what do they cost apiece?"

"Three *øre*—but, Lord! that's nothing to them at all. No, you should have seen the order that came in the day they had their garden party. *Five* cakes with icing and marzipan."

"Why, the bakers must be making a fortune."

"They've made it already. Mistress bought a new hat the other day."

"What was on it?" asked her mother. But her father leaned back with closed eyes, feeling as if his own thirst were assuaged for the moment by the flow of money Hedvig dipped her fingers in.

He was feverish, and needed something cooling. Here he was in the throes of his invention, and could not get it out.

Not a step nearer. No boat, nothing. And it was nearly autumn now. The trees stood there with their round juicy fruits. But, in his mind, it was all flowers. Was there anyone in all Knarreby so poor as the Egholms? Unless it were Bisserup, the brushmaker. And yet Egholm had spared no pains. He had tried Etatsraaden, tried Bro, the grocer, Rothe, the ironfounder; practically speaking, everyone of means in the place. He had also, by the way, tried those without means. Altogether, he had not passed by many an open ear without shouting into it something about Egholm's fore-and-aft turbine. Rothe had promised to make the castings for him, but that was all.

He looked at Hedvig. She stood up, reaching with her thin, girlish arms for the parcel with her white apron in, up on the dresser. Off to her work. Off to all that money again.

"Wait a minute," he said. There was a slight pause then, before he could stammer out his proposal—that they should all kneel down and pray to God. He did not know why, but it must be now, just at this moment, he said.

This was by no means a new and unheard-of thing; on the contrary, it had been known as far back as Hedvig could remember.

"It'll keep till this evening, won't it?" she said. "I shall be late if I stay behind now."

"'Seek first the kingdom of God and righteousness....'"

"Ha!" A single sound, like the scream of a cockerel, escaped from Hedvig. It was the first time she had openly derided her father's godliness. She regretted it bitterly next moment. True, the door out to the alley-way was open, just at her left, but what was the good of escaping herself when her mother was left behind to face what would come? She knew what it was to come home in high spirits from her work, and find her mother weeping, perhaps bruised into the bargain. She had no wish to experience that again.

The tears were gathering already; something was choking her.

Egholm set his hands on the arms of his chair, to spring up and dash out into the kitchen, but his anger seemed to snap in the middle.

In a sudden glimpse of vision he saw Hedvig in a new light. The slip of a girl, whose naughtinesses he had been at such pains to weed out, was no longer a slip of a girl and merely naughty—she was a *sinner*.

Every line of her figure, every feature in her face spoke blasphemy. She stood there with the challenge of an idol.

With a strangely sweet horror her father noted all: her guilty mouth, half-open, with lips pale and narrow, yet fresh, and teeth white as almonds, whence issued that hell-born defiance. Her blood must be evil as smoking brimstone.

Egholm sank back powerless in his chair.

But a moment later a new feeling came over him. How great a thing would it be to bring this child of sin to God, with bowed head and folded hands. "There is more joy in heaven over one sinner that repenteth, than of the ninety and nine which need no repentance." So the Scripture said. Hedvig would be a heavenly subject for conversion.

And there could be no doubt but that God would appreciate the efforts of the one who had borne the trial of that conversion.

Hedvig stood with her back to him, slightly stooping, as if awaiting the blow. She started when her father came out and laid his hand on her shoulder instead.

The conversion process appeared strangely easy; yes, she should always find something to say to the bakers by way of excuse. She set to work at once pulling the chairs aside to make room.

Her father looked crestfallen and unsatisfied. He had been prepared for a struggle—but this was *too* easy.

Still, he had something in reserve. Little Emanuel, whose inconsiderable length of days might serve as warrant for his innocence, was set on a pillow in the middle of the floor.

"Put something under your knees, Hedvig dear," said her mother.

"No need of that," said Egholm, thumping his own on the floor with unnecessary force.

"Oh, great and merciful God...."

"You've got your hat on, dear," said Fru Egholm mildly.

He sent her a wrathful glance, but laid aside his hat with much dignity.

"Almighty God, Lord of Heaven and Earth...."

Egholm's prayer began as a sonorous commonplace, an echo from the halls of the Brethren of St. John. But gradually, as his subject grew on him, his own individual religious view for the time being showed through.

It was to God as the Owner of great possessions that he prayed.

If any had asked him who was the greatest inventor in the world, he would have confessed, with a pious bend of the head, that it was one of the least of God's servants, an unworthy creature by the name of Egholm. But at the thought that God *owned* the fields, the woods, and the cities—the lands and the seas, Egholm, who had never owned more than the poor clothes he wore and a trifle of old furniture, was moved to prostrate himself before that mighty power.

It distressed him, however, that God should suffer those possessions of His to be put to ill use, in that He allowed them to fall into the wrong hands. It was by no means altogether selfishness that led him, Egholm, here to point out himself as one who would be a true and grateful steward of even the largest and most troublesome estate.

"Am I not Thy son, art Thou not my Father, whose will it is that all should be well with me?"

Hedvig heard but little of her father's words: her eyes were following the hands of the clock; it was jerking by tiny stages on towards twelve. There it stopped, and seemed to linger for a moment, as if inviting the figure to join it on its way; then on again, irrevocably on and on. She clenched her teeth in impotent fury. Then suddenly a new note was touched in her father's prayer—something which made her all attention.

He had commenced, quite advisedly, with the practical human tactics of praising those qualities in the Lord which he himself wished to call forth towards himself.

"Thy goodness is without end and beyond all measure. So great is Thy love to us poor children of men, that Thou hearest every prayer we offer up to Thee, and grantest it. It is written: 'Ask, and thou shalt receive!' So great is Thy loving-kindness unto us, that Thou wouldst not have us suffer more, and therefore sayest, let there be an end. Behold, Egholm Thy servant groaneth under the weight of poverty; Thou seest, and it is enough; Thou sayest the word, and lo, Thy servant cometh into riches and happiness...."

The words seemed to have a sort of hypnotic power; for a moment, Hedvig quivered with hope that it might really come to pass. Then she remembered how often she had heard the same thing; how many times she had been forced to kneel thus on aching knees in prayer for the same, but to no avail. From the time she was first able to speak, her tongue had praised the Lord. Now, it revolted her; something within her seemed to rise in protest; she felt that she *hated* God.

Never for a moment did she doubt His existence; on the contrary, she seemed to see His face. But it was a face hard and cold as stone, with eyes looking absently out. The ardent prayers of men were powerless to affect Him.

She began mumbling an oath every time her father found a new form for his praise.

It was otherwise with Egholm himself. He felt stronger and stronger as he went on; and at sight of Hedvig's lips moving, he burst into tears, and found courage to speak out without reserve.

For it was a curious fact that more courage was needed to ask for little things. It was a simple matter enough to pray for wealth and happiness in general, but to-day he managed to get out the matter that really troubled him.

"Dear, good Lord, grant me—or only *lend* me—one hundred *kroner*; even fifty would do. You know what it's for—that boat, the green boat of Ulrik's. Not his new one, but the old. You know, dear Lord, I want it for my steam-turbine. And I've come to a dead stop now, and can't move a step if you won't lend me a miserable fifty *kroner*...."

His voice had altered now to a wheedling tone, with a marked city accent. He made a sort of half scrape-and-bow, and finished off.

"A—far...." prattled Emanuel.

It was Egholm's habit after a prayer to embrace his wife. He made as if to do so now, but, to his surprise, she thrust him away with every indication of ill-will.

"No! Don't think you're going to get me on to that sort of thing, because I won't."

"That sort of thing!" Egholm's voice was uncertain; he had a feeling that his wife was, after all, somehow in relation with the heavenly powers.

"No good having a cow that yields when it kicks over the bucket after. The first part was all right, but if you think God's going to help with your silly tricks about that turbine thing—why, you're very much mistaken."

"But, why not?..."

"Because it's an abomination. Cain was the first smith, and you know it. And the Lord hates all that hammering and smithying about at turbines and steam carts and friction cylinders…."

"Friction couplings," corrected Egholm gently.

"Well, I don't care what you call them. He hates all that sort of stuff, whatever name you give it. And you can be certain sure you'll get nothing out of that prayer," she concluded, with a lofty shake of her head.

Egholm sat down in silence, and Hedvig, seeing that he was overcome by some incomprehensible means, hurried off in relief.

What had come to Egholm now? Was he impressed by his wife's wisdom? Oh, he thought her foolish beyond words.

But she had destroyed his exaltation as effectively as a knife thrust into a balloon.

His head dropped on his breast.

Yes, it was true enough, no doubt, that God was against him in all his plans and inventions. His prayer had been in vain, despite the brilliant idea of bringing along Hedvig as a sacrifice.

"Well, what do you think I ought to do?" he asked weakly.

"Me! And how's a simple creature like me to say what you should do? You're so clever…."

He fancied there was something behind her words, and grasped at it eagerly.

"What d'you mean?"

Fru Egholm kept up her pretence of emptiness for some time, but her speech was crafty as a will-o'-the-wisp, and he followed her till he lost his foothold. Then she said:

"Write to the Brethren, and ask for your money back."

Egholm looked up with a momentary gleam of light, but pursed up his mouth in a grimace, and said:

"The Brethren—no. I've done with them for good and all."

"All right, then, just as you please," said she. And no more was said.

Towards evening, Egholm took his stick, and went for a walk through the town and down along the quay.

The black gliding waters of the Belt slapped softly against the stonework, and patted like flat hands under the tarred beams. He went right out to the point, where some boys were fishing with lines, and calling to one another in their singing dialect, as often as they fancied a bite.

A big Norwegian timber ship with a heavy deck-load lay in the harbour, and all the fishing-boats of Knarreby were gathered along the side of the quay.

The background was dominated by the church, the Custom House, and Vang's hotel. To the west, little fisher huts set all up a steep slope, that rose farther on to the great beeches of Kongeskoven. Knarreby itself was on an elevation; the ground line of St. Nicholas Church was level with the roof of the Custom House. From where he stood, Egholm could see two gravestones showing white in the churchyard.

Loud voices could be heard from the terrace of Vang's hotel; three gentlemen had just come out, and were sniffing and wiping their foreheads with handkerchiefs. Evidently, they had been dining. Somebody gave an order to a waiter, with a heavy slap on the back. There was a certain noisiness apparent.

Egholm pricked up his ears—that was Rothe's voice and no other.

Ah—and now he recognised the other two: the warlike editor and Vang with a silk skull-cap.

Here were three men who, he felt sure, never bowed the knee to God. And yet they seemed to enjoy themselves.

How could it be?

That fellow Rothe, for instance, the ironfounder. He was said to have started at the lowest rung, as a blacksmith's hand, eighteen years ago. Now, he owned the whole of Knarreby ironfoundry.

A turbine boat would be a mere nothing to a man like that.

Egholm sat on the quay for a while, following the three with envious eyes; then he strolled in towards the land with the ferrule of his stick dragging listlessly over the stones.

There was the usual crowd of fishermen gathered about the warehouse. They were always to be found there or over by the agent's house. The walls of both were worn smooth by the backs of their trousers.

"Going to have thunder?" asked Egholm, with a swinging gesture which he fancied smacked of the sea.

They puffed at their pipes, and squinted in towards the centre, where

Peder Kvabs stood. He was the fattest and reddest-faced of them all, and went about in his shirt-sleeves all the year round. When he said nothing, then there was nothing to be said.

Well, after all, no need for any introduction, thought Egholm, and came to the matter of his turbine at once. Funny thing, when you came to think of it, that in four or five years from now every little rowing-boat would have its turbine, and go spurting across the Belt like a cat, dead against the wind.

"If only it don't turn out one of them infernal machines like they use for the Czar," said Peder Kvabs, spitting between his teeth. The others were roused at his words to some considerable emotion. They rubbed themselves against the wooden wall, spat, and worked their eyebrows up and down. One of them made strange sounds.

"Ah, well," said Egholm, discomfited, "you wait and see."

He walked a few paces, swinging his stick, then turned and called back to them:

"You wait and see when it comes! I'm getting the money now—three or four hundred *kroner*. From Odense. It's money I was done out of under false pretences. And I'm going to have the law of them...."

The woollen jerseys seemed to betray a seething and bubbling within. The men could contain themselves no longer. Suddenly Peder Kvabs hoisted his slacks, and led the whole flock hastily into the nearest *café*. There was no need to ask should they go; all felt it was a simple necessity.

"Yes," said Egholm to himself. "That's what I'll do. They couldn't give it against me if I went to law."

But he felt sorely in need of someone who would have faith in him, and he longed for Henrik Vang's ever-ready admiration. Might just slip up to his room....

Fru Vang kept a quiet little boarding-house for a few old bachelors who had taken the best rooms of the house. She and Vang himself occupied separate attics.

Vang was in bed, with half an inch of reddish stubble on his chin, and the hair on his forehead clammy with feverish sweat.

"Why, what's this?" cried Egholm, aghast. "Are you ill? And I'd never heard a word.... A great strong fellow like you! What's the matter?"

"Sit down a minute," said Vang faintly. "We can shift this here. Or give it to Diana ... there you are."

He set a plate down on the floor, and wiped the seat of a chair with his bare arm.

"I've worked it out," said Egholm, without preface. "The boiler must be vertical. With the first experimental boat, of course, it's more than ever important to save space. Can't make out why I didn't hit on that before."

There were half a score of other things he had "worked out." Vang listened attentively, wrinkling up his forehead and gazing ceilingwards, as if something were passing far above his head.

Egholm felt comfortable now, and in a burst of geniality exclaimed:

"Here, Vang, you'd better let me have a look at you. I'm something of a doctor—natural healer, you know. I was patching up Madam Hermansen's leg the other day. Have you seen a doctor at all? What did he say?"

"No, I haven't," said Vang, looking away.

"All the better; nothing to distract my instinctive powers. Where's the pain?"

"Oh, you know all the time," said Vang piteously, laying one hand on Egholm's arm. "Don't go teasing me now, there's a good fellow."

Egholm rose to his feet in surprise; his imagination was weaving intricate tangles in a moment.

"Is it—is it.... No, I've no idea—really, I haven't."

Vang pouted like a boy, and after a little hesitation explained that his wife had a habit now and again—more and more frequently of late—of taking away his trousers. He had been lying here now for four days, with no trousers to put on.

"Oh, don't sit there grinning just like all the rest of them!"

"I'm not, indeed. So she takes away your trousers? First-rate idea, you know, really. She's one of my sort. But, look here, you know, we must be able to borrow a pair from somewhere. I've only these myself, more's the pity. But we might take it in turns...."

"There's only one man in the place whose trousers fit me. And he won't. Oh, the beast! I sent down to ask him. He knows very well what's the trouble. It's Rothe."

There was a sound of short, rapid steps outside. Vang listened, waved one arm as if with a baton to bid the orchestra cease, and fell back, looking very ill indeed. There was a knock, and Fru Vang entered. She was a dark, thin, sour-looking woman with pale cheeks and a burnt fringe.

Vang sat up hastily and made the introduction with an ease of manner acquired from habitual attendance at ballrooms, then lay back and resumed his invalid air.

"I've sewed that button on," said Fru Vang, laying something on the bed. "Don't you think you might try to get up now?"

She tripped back and forth about her husband's bed, settled his pillows, and pulled the sheet straight. Her skirts were shorter than was usual, and her patent shoes had pointed toes and very high heels.

The legs were undoubtedly the legs of a waitress, but the rest of her was unimpeachable. Save, perhaps, for the fringe.... Yes, the legs and the fringe....

Egholm left the pair to themselves and hurried home. He had gained something at least, in that his gloomy thoughts were dispersed for the time being. Again and again he stopped, shook his head, and snorted with laughter, at the recollection of huge Vang's helpless expression.

After all, there was no sense in taking things too seriously. Most of life was only fooling at the best. He would write to the Brethren, yes; but he would not be a fool and insist on his rights; much better to go warily, and beg their assistance in his extremity. It was one of the rules of the community to help any brother in distress.

Fru Egholm had the pleasure of her husband's company till late that night. She looked to her work, and he sat there as in the old days, busy with pen and ink and quantities of paper. But he was not angry now; he hummed and chuckled in a self-satisfied way. At one o'clock he began to read his petition aloud.

The letter ought to be sent off at once, wherefore he started off himself to the railway station, and Fru Egholm was for once the first to retire. She was asleep when he returned, but woke shortly after, and was puzzled a good deal by a curious sniffling sound that seemed to come from his pillow. Then the bed shook, and all at once she realised that he was laughing!

Ah, well, those who laugh at night may come to weep by day, she thought to herself, with some irritation.

Egholm gabbled away for some time about the turbine, about his letter to the Brethren, and about Vang, the trouserless, and his wife.

His wife.... Ah, she was a devil! A cold air seemed to breathe from her —though she might well have exhaled overmuch warmth in earlier days. He remembered her mechanical smile and her soft, gentle ministrations about her husband's bedside. False, false from top to toe.

One might almost be tempted to say that there was but one thing genuine about her—her false teeth! Egholm ducked down in bed again at the thought, his lips opening and closing stickily.

XVI

The Egholms managed to drag on into December without using their stove.

Fru Egholm pointed to the trees in Andreasen's garden, showing how the leaves broke away in the frost, and slid drowning one by one down through the air, like naked yellowish bodies.

"Well, and what then?" asked her husband uncomprehendingly.

"Why, then—it's winter, and time to be getting in fuel, unless you want to perish with cold."

"Why, as for that," said Egholm, leaning over the kitchen table to get a better view, "there's one tree there that's as green as ever. Look."

"Green as ever it may be," said his wife, "seeing it's an evergreen. That's holly."

"Holly's a sacred tree," said Egholm, "and we should take it as a model." It was not meant in jest. He really endeavoured to school himself to endurance. He left one button of his coat undone, and made long speeches about the unwarrantable luxury of having a fire in the stove. When you went about wrapped up in clothes, and even lived in a house, why....

Fru Egholm sighed. She made herself and Emanuel into bundles of clothes, and hoped for the best.

At first it really seemed as if Egholm had conquered the ancient prejudice in favour of warmth. He talked about pawning his overcoat, and went about rejoicing at his excellent health. He expected to feel even better as it grew colder, he said.

But cold was a strangely elusive enemy to fight against. Out in the open, in a gale of wind, where one might expect to find it at its worst, he could defeat it easily, and come home flushed and warm. Then, before he knew it, it had crushed and left him exhausted in his own comparatively sheltered room. His wrists grew thinner, and his fingers curled like the fingers of a corpse.

One evening he gave in completely. Now he *would* have a fire, and that at once. And since there was nothing else in the place to burn, he cut up his wife's chopping-boards, tore out the stuffing from an old straw mattress, and trampled Hedvig's doll's house flat. Fru Egholm made piteous protest, but Hedvig simply looked on with a curious smile. Next day Egholm himself was most eager to obtain credit at the coal merchant's.

This, then, was the state of things in the house. They had no money, and very little credit; both difficult things to do without.

People seemed to have forgotten there was such a thing as having their photograph taken.

The Egholms felt it in various ways: food and clothing, for instance. Hedvig could manage all right as to food. She was always eating at the baker's, and cakes dropped out of her clothes when she undressed at night; she brought them home for Emanuel. But even her existence was touched with the ugly grey brush of poverty. Her boots were a marvel; every schoolgirl in the town knew Hedvig's boots. They had an extraordinary number of buttons up the side, with springs, and a sort of ventilation. They must have cost a great deal at one time. There were no soles to them now, but that did not matter, said her father—you don't walk with your feet in the air! Hedvig admitted there was something in that, and comforted herself further with the thought that no one could see what her under things were like.

There was little gaiety about the Egholms' life.

And yet there was one little being whose only longing day and night was to share their lot in every way. This was Sivert in his smithy.

The day his mother had got into the train and glided out into the morning mist, his organ of equilibrium had suffered a shock. One day he would fall, and fall, moreover, in the direction of Knarreby.

He had always been keenly attached to his mother, and, now that she was gone, his longing conjured up her picture into this or that piece of bright metal he held, or he would hear her voice in the blowing of the bellows. Then he would laugh and talk out loud, or stand up and swing his arms in a joyful embrace towards his beloved mother.

Whereupon his master would immediately land out at him from one side, and Olsen from the other, which was perhaps the reason why he retained the same degree of crookedness.

His mother had given him to understand that there would be occasional visits; either he should come to Knarreby, or she would come to him there, but there came nothing more than a letter once a month, and even these grew shorter and shorter. At last they contained hardly more than the advice to be a good boy and do what he was told, and not to forget his prayers.

Sivert read them with quivering mouth, and nodded; he would do as she said.

Then, further, the letter reported that they were all well at home. Sivert nodded at this likewise. But when he came to read the signature, "Your own loving mother," the tears began to trickle down, and, a moment after, he was sobbing all over.

Each day was for the boy a ladder of a hundred toilsome steps, and the ladder led to nights spent with Olsen. It was getting on towards Christmas. Sivert realised it one day, as he came trotting along through the street with a load of iron rods.

In one of the shop windows stood a Christmas tree decked out with little baskets and paper horns and cottonwool on all the branches. There was a crowd of children in front of the window. Sivert made a sharp turn about, and stood there lost in admiration. Ho! That was a Christmas tree! He knew it!

He was not suffered to stand there very long, for his iron rods barred the whole footway. But for the rest of his journey back, he talked out loud to himself of the wonderful vision.

It *was* a Christmas tree. Then Christmas must be coming. It was put in the window as a sign that Christmas would soon be here.

Already there was a taste of sweets in his mouth, just as he remembered once before....

Then suddenly his mother's letters, that he knew by heart, began talking too.

"All well at home!"

At home—yes, at home ... with Mother, they were all well.

An indomitable craving, and a resolution, ripened within him.

His craving was that he, too, would share in that "all well" at home. As to the resolution, he clenched his teeth upon it for the present, and his eyes stared fixedly. In the evening, when he had seen Olsen go out, he stood with shaking hands up in their room, and collected his belongings. Yes, this was what he was going to do. He was going home. And never come back any more. So he must be careful not to forget a single thing.

There were his pictures all cut out, his letters and—under the mattress—that indispensable tie-pin given him by the Eriksens at his confirmation; he would find some use for it, no doubt, when he was older.

And that was all. But still he wandered about the room, looking into every corner.

In the washstand drawer was Olsen's registration book—fancy Olsen's leaving it there! Suppose a thief....

In a moment of confusion, Sivert's hand dipped into the drawer, closed all five fingers on the book, and thrust it under his blouse, close against his trembling heart.

Then, overcome by dizziness, he stole on all fours down the stairs.

The shop windows were ablaze, and the streets full of people. It was all like some great festival, thought Sivert, as he trotted along in the gutter.

Suddenly it struck him that he might encounter Olsen.

Wasn't that Olsen coming round the corner there? Sivert did not stay to make closer investigation, but raced off down the first turning. And there—Heaven preserve him!—was Olsen himself, coming out of a tavern not ten paces away. It *was* Olsen this time. Leaning up against the railing just as Olsen always did. Sivert turned round and fled, as if the lightnings of retribution were at his heels, dodging in a zigzag through a maze of intercrossing streets.

He came into quarters of the town where he had never been before, and met four more Olsens on his way. Once with a girl on his arm, once in the very gateway where he was hiding in fear of—yes, of that same Olsen.

At last he found the road he sought—the road to Knarreby. The distance between the houses increased, and the gale rose to a hurricane. It was full in his face now, and beating against his cheeks with a torrent of sand and stones, but he bent forward and drew his cap down over his eyes, sighting at the next lamp-post through the split between the peak and the cloth top, and keeping his hands behind his back.

Yes, he would manage it now!

Then suddenly there were no more lamp-posts to go by. The last one shed its gleam a few yards round, a solitary figure of a lamp, the extreme outpost, rattling its glass with a noise as of chattering teeth in the cold, and its flame hopping from the wick at every gust. Sivert set his back against it—he dared not give himself up entirely to the gaping jaws of the black dark ahead.

He knew the place well, by the way; he had stood here many a Sunday afternoon, staring out towards Knarreby. The tears welled up chokingly within him now.

A little later, there came a man with a pole. He growled out something or other, but Sivert drew away shyly out of the ring of light.

Well, well, the man put out the lamp, and turned in towards the town again, leaving darkness behind him as he went.

Sivert stole on behind him, sobbing. The putting out of the lamps entered into his consciousness as a picture of his own desolation.

Late that night he squeezed himself up in the doorway of the old home in Nedergade, where he had not been since his mother left.

The gloomy place had something of homeliness about it; almost instinctively he stole in through the door to the washing cellar. There were tubs lying about, full of washing left to soak.

He stumbled in amongst them, and took a drink of water from the tap, not so much from thirst, but more from a fancy to use his familiar knowledge of the place. Then he recollected that it made a buzzing sound in the tenements upstairs when that tap was turned on, and he hurried away to the passage between the coal cellars. Egholms' cellar used to be the fifth. Could he manage now to tear open the padlock with a smart twist? Wonderful—it was as easy as ever! That showed that God was with him after all. Full of thankfulness, Sivert slipped into the narrow space, and tried to concentrate his mind on the Lord's Prayer, but fell asleep despite his efforts, and did not wake until the pale light of morning came filtering in to him through the cobwebbed windows. His back was like a boil from the knobs and points of the firewood he had been lying on.

Out in the washing cellars someone was rattling tubs and buckets, and the water was running.

Sivert pressed himself closer up in a corner. He stood there a long time, till his sense was dulled. There was a bottle in the window, that looked as if it had been used for oil. A cork was stuck half-way down the neck. And from among the broken lumps of peat and turf on the floor a lump of old iron pipe was sticking out.

Sivert looked at the two things—first one, then the other, a hundred times. Bottle—iron pipe—iron pipe—bottle. He thrust out his wooden shoe and kicked at the pipe to make a change. There was a brass tap on it. It emerged from the litter on the floor like a revelation.

"Father's big tap," he burst out in wondering recognition. They must have forgotten it. No, not forgotten; it had been left here for him to take with him.

Half an hour later he was clattering along at a sharp trot out of the town, with the tap under his coat.

The poplars stood in two endless rows with their leafless branches pointing stiffly heavenwards. Only one thing to do now—get along as fast as he could. His heart might hop and thump as it pleased, like a dry nut in its shell; he had no use for that now—only for his legs.

Villages showed up ahead of him and faded away behind, all nothing to do with him. It did not enter his head to ask for food anywhere, or even to rest. Only go on, on, along the road, past ditches where the snow lay streaked with wind-borne dust, and tufts of withered grass above; past flattened heaps of road-metal that lay like so many nameless graves. Trotting or dragging his feet, he went on past buzzing telegraph poles, passing or following heavy-laden milk-carts or solitary peasants with kerchiefs bound over their ears as a protection from the biting cold.

He spoke to no one until evening was drawing on; then, an old woman told him there was but another mile to Knarreby.

This came to him as something of a shock; he felt there ought to be, say, four or six miles more yet.

He slackened his pace, and at the same time his mind began working again.

All the way till now, through those twenty-four icy miles, he had had a feeling that he was running straight into his mother's welcoming arms. Now the picture changed incomprehensibly. Her open arms were turned to clenched fists, and her gentle eyes gave place to his father's glaring fiery orbs. After all, perhaps it was not so simple a matter to run away from one's place and go home!

Thrashings, even kicks, he knew, but how should he ever be able to bear his father's thundering voice when he was angry? Sivert remembered how he had once himself offered his father a brass ladle to beat him with, just to get it over. His father had taken it—yes—and there were dints in it still. Oh, his father's voice was the most terrible thing in the world. It was not thick like Olsen's, or whinnying like the smith's, but a sort of voice that made one feel stiff all over.

By the time he reached Knarreby Mill it was pitch dark. The high invisible sails flung rattling round past a little red window far above. A little later, and the town itself blinked out to meet him, but it was some time before he managed, with the help of a lad of his own age, to find the way in through Andreasen's yard, and stood, with beating heart, looking in at the light behind the familiar green curtains. Someone was standing outside the window, looking in from one side where the curtain was folded. Someone in a blue blouse, only a little bigger than Sivert himself. He did not look so very dangerous.... When Sivert crept nearer, the other started, as if to run away, but judging Sivert to be equally harmless, he thought better of it, and soon the two had come to a whispered understanding.

The figure in the blue blouse was called Marinus. Yes, and Sivert could stand there by the other window, if he liked, and look in, if he kept quite still.

Inside, was Mother—yes, his mother—sitting over her work, making up hair. Her practised fingers took up the piece, plaited it into the three strands, thrust it into place, and then, wetting her fingers, she reached for another. She nodded now and then as she worked. And the lamp was reflected upside down in her spectacles.

Sivert began sniffing and swallowing something in his throat. Then he tore himself away from that picture, and perceived his father sitting in a big arm-chair, his fingers twined into his beard, reading the Bible. Now he turned a page; now he lifted his eyes from the book and fixed something or other in space, nailing it, as it were, to the ceiling with his glance.

On the settee in the room behind, the light from the lamp shone on Emanuel's fair round head, and by the door sat Hedvig, undressed, combing her hair. She had drawn one leg up under her, and leaned back dreamily. A feeling of envy stole over Sivert at sight of those legs, so thick and overfed they seemed, both here and there. And both legs, too—oh, it was not fair.

Truly, all well at home.

His father was speaking. Hedvig answered, but with lips tight and straight as a line, though her nose moved.

"Won't?" cried her father. "You disobedient little devil! To bed with you this instant!"

He slapped down the Bible on the table and shook his hand in the air.

"That's Father's voice; I know it. I know it's the right one," muttered Sivert. His legs carried him staggering out through the gateway again, and Marinus turned and watched him as he went.

After much aimless wandering, Sivert found his way at last into the waiting-room of the railway station. It was naturally his last resource, being the only place that showed a light still burning.

His wooden shoes echoed in the empty room, but no one came to turn him out. He slept close to a lovely warm stove, and heard trains rushing past, doors opening and slamming through his sleep; not till next morning did anyone disturb him, and then it was an old peasant who slipped the boy's feet down to make room for himself on the bench. There were a number of other people about.

One or two men in heavy travelling cloaks walked up and down, rubbing their hands for warmth. A waitress with beautiful frills at her throat had appeared; she took down the shutters from the buffet and set out dishes of refreshments. A little later came the popping of corks.

Vehicles rolled up outside; and drivers with silver-tasseled hats came in and hung over the bar. They talked with noisy humour of the waitress, who, they declared, looked as if she had not slept well that night. The lady in question, however, merely raised her eyebrows to show that she had not even heard what they said. Now and again she scratched her hair with the least little touch of one fourth finger. Sivert understood this as evidence that so elegant a being had little need to scratch at all.

Altogether, it was a morning rich in experience for Sivert. When the trains and the passengers had gone, the head-scratching waitress sat down to further cups of coffee. Sivert shifted a little closer, and saw how deliciously ready to hand were the dishes of *smørrebrød*,[4] whereat his mouth watered quite literally, down his blouse.

"Are you going by train?"

"No," said Sivert, dismayed at being noticed. Doubtless he would be turned out at once.

"What are you doing, then?" said the waitress after a pause. She was taking her hair down, and undoing the plaits.

What was he doing? Heaven only knew!

"Taking home the big tap. For Father," he stammered.

The lady laughed—it sounded like a scream. A moment after she was serious again, but anyhow, she *had* laughed. She was sitting now, bending forward, combing her back hair upward and forward in little jerks, and observing the effect in a little round mirror with an advertisement on the back. She laughed, though it evidently hurt badly when the comb stuck.

A lovely creature, was that waitress.

"And who's your father?"

"Egholm. I saw him eat one of those once. Just like that." Sivert nodded sideways towards the dish.

"One of what?"

"One of those!" said Sivert, springing up to the counter and pointing to a piece with slices of sausage. "This one's bigger, though, I'm sure."

Sivert could not say more; he stammered and hiccuped in a delirium of hunger.

The waitress was combing back again now, till the comb fairly crackled;

she spread out her chest mightily, and shook her mane of hair.

"You can have that piece, if you like," she said, with her mouth full of hairpins. And added mysteriously: "Serve her right, too."

Three further pieces were granted Sivert on the same grounds, of serving somebody right. He laughed and cried and stuffed his mouth all at the same time.

"You're a funny sort of deaf-and-dumb lad, you are. What's your name?"

"Well, I'm mostly Olsen, really," said Sivert, fumbling at the place where the precious book was hidden. "But I'm not all deaf and dumb. Not quite...."

"Well, I said you were half a lunatic."

"... Or I couldn't sing, you know."

"Let's hear you sing." The barmaiden surveyed her work of art in its entirety, until it seemed as if her eyes would turn back to front in their sockets.

"Well, I can, you know...." said Sivert hesitatingly.

The barmaid pointed to another piece—cheese it was this time—with her little finger. Sivert pounced on it at once.

Then he wiped his mouth, wrinkled up his forehead thoughtfully, and rattled off at a furious rate:

"The pretty bird upon the tree its merry notes doth sing...."

and all the rest of that verse. It sounded like an Eskimo letting off a single word of a hundred syllables or so.

"That wasn't singing, not yet; I was just trying if I knew all the words," explained Sivert apologetically, and proceeded to repeat the words "with music."

A porter and one or two others came up, and grouped themselves in an attentive half-circle about the singing mannikin.

Sivert sang all the *smørrebrød* off one dish, and then went out with the porter to a little room where they cleaned the lamps, and here he talked of many remarkable things, helping to clean lamps the while. At last he brought out his brass tap, and polished that up till it shone. Then suddenly he stole off unobserved.

Down the street and across Andreasen's yard, walking awkwardly and shuffling like an epileptic, his mouth running over all the time with prayers and verses of hymns.

In the little entry he stood still and laid one ear to the crack of the door, listening breathlessly.

Yes, there was Emanuel prattling away, and his mother answering with a few low words.

Was it to be his luck to find them alone? He listened again, with his head on one side, and heard now another sound—a long-drawn, sucking sound, almost like a snore, and then the rattle of a cup, repeated at regular intervals. Ah … now he knew who was there besides!

Sivert knelt down where he stood, with his face against the door and his hands folded piously. He had knelt that way once before, when he had happened to upset a lamp. So, too, Knud, the Martyr-King, had knelt waiting for death. It was the proper thing on such occasions, and no doubt looked well. But was his hair all right?

He drew forth the brass tap, and tried to make out his own reflection swimming unsteadily in the polished metal.

Perhaps he had spoken aloud. For suddenly his father appeared in the open door. The first astonishment in his face changed to inflamed fury, and he swung back his boot ready for a blow.

Sivert, terrified, held up the brass tap like a crucifix above his head, as if to guard.

His thoughts were scattered in flight like sparrows at a shot, but some instinct came to his aid, and he cried out in his cracked voice, echoing through the house:

"Oh, Lord my God, I've brought your brass tap."

Sivert's ideas as to his father on earth and his Father in heaven had always been somewhat vague; now, they seemed fused into one.

The effect of his words was beyond comprehension. The threatened kick did not fall; his father snatched up the tap instead, and said:

"Wherever did you find it? I've been wanting it all the time."

"In the cellar," said Sivert. "But it wasn't me that didn't bring it along."

And with an idiot laugh he collapsed in his mother's arms.

Egholm stood by the window overlooking the yard. He blew through the tap, and turned it lovingly in his fingers. A great ship came throbbing towards him and took him on board. And he mounted up, high, high, up to the bridge.

"Full speed ahead! Stand by! Full speed astern!"

And the ship went astern till Captain Egholm felt the tears welling into his eyes with delight. A little after, he went to the kitchen door.

"Sivert!"

A timorous "Yes" came from within.

"Did you really think I was God Himself?"

Sivert nodded.

His father turned on his heel and said calmly:

"Then you were wrong, boy, because I'm not."

XVII

Egholm went up to the station in a great state of excitement every time a train was due from Odense. There had come a wondrous letter in a blue envelope from the Brethren there—a document to the effect that the community had voted him a gift of money. It would be delivered in person within a few days, by Evangelist Karlsen.

The letter lay on the floor, as if deposited by mysterious means from above. And certainly no one had heard the postman come.

Egholm gave thanks to God. That was a thing which should be done to the full, and preferably a little before the fulfilment of his prayer.

For the first few days he talked a great deal about the practice he had gradually acquired in the art of prayer. But as Karlsen still failed to appear, he grew silent, and began going up to meet the trains. And then at last, on the eighth day, just as he came home tired and discouraged from the station, there sat the Evangelist himself in the parlour.

He, too, looked as if some angel had brought him on wings through the air, though, as a matter of fact, this was not the case. He explained himself that he had come by train from Jutland.

Egholm forgot to take off his coat; he sat down opposite his ancient enemy, lacking words with which to begin. And, truth to tell, he was humiliated and abashed after all at having to accept a gift, in view of what had passed. What made things worse was that the Evangelist was grown so surpassingly elegant in his dress. No more butcher-boots—nothing like it. Striped trousers he wore, and a smart-looking collar and cuffs. True, the last were of indiarubber, but still.... His moustache was simply beyond description, and the blue-black wether-eyes glittered like globes of lightning. Under his chair was a handbag, undeniably new, but, of course, ... no, of course, it couldn't be the money in that.

Karlsen looked round the room, and thrust his shoulders back, as if preparing to speak, but still he did not seem to find the suitable "word."

What was he to say? As for the gift, that could wait a little. A sermon would hardly do either, though he was known to be a first-rate hand at that. Suppose he were to launch out with a suitable text? Yes, that would be the thing!

Karlsen went about, so to speak, with his pockets full of texts, which he used, now to smite the head of an unruly disciple, now to scatter like golden largesse among the poor. He had, too, long extracts from Revelations, which could be flung like lassos to entangle the ungodly, cooling draughts from the Sermon on the Mount, and blood and fire from the Mosaic portions of the Old Testament. But it always took a certain degree of opposition before he could be brought to use them.

Egholm asked in a very general way how the Brotherhood was getting on.

"First-rate," said Karlsen, with an absent yawn—"first-rate," and relapsed into silence.

Egholm could not keep away from the scene of the crime. He stammered out:

"Karlsen, you mustn't regard my attack—my somewhat over-zealous attack, perhaps—that evening, you know, as—as evidence of enmity towards the Brethren. Not in the least. There was much in the Brotherhood that I greatly appreciated. A certain simplicity.... No; if hard words were said, they were due to a momentary indignation over the refusal to give me a plain, straightforward answer to my definite question, regarding that text in the Epistle to the Hebrews, which—at any rate to my humble mind—expressly annuls all giving of tithes."

Karlsen gloated awhile over Egholm's downcast eyes and the tip of his tongue creeping over dry lips. He wrinkled up his forehead deeply, and said, with that crafty, ingratiating smile that was so thoroughly his own:

"An answer, my dear friends—why, of course. Nothing easier. You shall have it to-day. I've a big fat book here in my bag; you can read it there to your heart's content...."

"A book?..."

"Yes. Half a minute, I'll show you. Six *kroner's* the price of it, but there's edifying reading for more than twice the money. Guaranteed. A big fat book, bound cloth boards. Let me show you."

"No, no. I'll take your word for it. No doubt it's excellent. But ... er ... well...."

It would be sheer madness to offend Karlsen now, and send him away with the three or four hundred *kroner*, but still, there was no sense in spending the six *kroner* if it could be helped. Egholm knew the book well enough himself—a rambling translation from the English.

"But ... er ... well, you know, there was nothing said about that on the night. If only they'd given me an answer in some way or other, I'm sure I'd never have resigned from the Brotherhood at all."

"You never did resign from the Brotherhood!"

"Well, no, not resigned exactly ... that is to say...."

Egholm sat crushed and despairing in the arm-chair, letting Karlsen do with him as he pleased.

"No, my dear good man, what possessed you to say so? If you weren't a disciple still, of course we shouldn't have troubled to help you. Nothing to do with us, you understand. As it is, why, we hung up a box for you at the meeting."

Egholm sighed inaudibly, and inwardly reduced his claim to half. So they had hung up a collecting box for him. Well, well. He knew those boxes. There were a number of them—hung along the wall like a row of young birds with hungrily gaping mouths. He remembered how the Evangelist used to draw attention to them discreetly before closing the proceedings for each evening—quite unnecessarily, by the way, seeing that Karlsen senior, the Angel of the flock, stood with hand outstretched in farewell, just where the boxes began.

"And now, my dear friends, we have heard the Word, for our souls' good, and that we can take with us in our hearts. And, in return, let us not forget to put something in the boxes. No one calls upon you to give much. When each gives what he can, it is enough. The first is for the hall, that we may have a place to meet in; the second is for light and firing—neither of these can be got for nothing, my dear friends—and the third is for myself—I need hardly remind you, my dear friends, that I cannot live on air. The fourth is for members of the Brotherhood in distress, and the fifth towards the purchase of a library. Put a little in each, and your conscience will be at ease!"

On tithe nights the boxes were not in evidence.

Egholm remembered that according to an unwritten law it was permissible to pass by the boxes for Brethren in distress and for the library. How would it have been with the sixth in the row, hung up for Egholm in the throes of poverty?

"Did any of them give anything?" he asked humbly.

"Oh, it brought in quite a lot," said Karlsen comfortably. "Quite a decent little sum. You see"—he leaned forward confidentially and plucked at Egholm's coat collar, almost stupefying him with his tobacco-laden breath—"I got the old man to stand beside it!"

He gave Egholm a friendly shake, and laughed in a spluttering shower.

"But there's one condition. I may as well tell you that first as last. The condition of your receiving this gift is, that your wife becomes a member of the Brotherhood. Both of you, you understand—or no gift! For it's her fault we've had all this bother about you. Yes, I've found that out. She's from Aalborg. I know those obstinate Jutland folk!"

"My wife!" cried Egholm. New difficulties towered before him at the idea, but, at the same time, the value of the gift seemed to increase. He sprang to his feet, and ran to the kitchen door.

"Well, there you are. Now you can talk it over with her," said Karlsen, with a laugh, leaning his head back and showing the scar of his "glands" and his ill-shaven throat. "But, look here, tell her at the same time I'm staying till the eight o'clock train, so you'll have to find me a bite of something to eat. You know what it says about us Evangelists: we're to have neither scrip nor staff, but take that which is set before us."

Fru Egholm was busy plaiting hair at the kitchen table. Her husband could see from the way she tugged at her work that she had followed the conversation in the next room.

"Never as long as I live," she said firmly.

A catastrophe seemed imminent, but Egholm was so destitute of physical or moral force at the moment that he contented himself with a threatening gesture.

"And as for supper," she went on, "wild horses wouldn't give us more than we've got, and that's no more than bread and dripping and a rind of cheese."

"Nothing hot—not even a cup of tea?"

"Only the clove."

"*Only* the clove! As if that wasn't good enough."

Clove tea was one of Egholm's minor inventions. One day when the tea and coffee canisters were as empty as his empty purse, he had manufactured an aromatic beverage from cloves and hot water. He himself drank it thereafter in quantities and with relish, and Sivert was for a time in his good books merely on account of the audible "Aaah!" which he gave when it was poured out. Fru Egholm, too, conceded that it was certainly cheap—a packet of cloves costing two *øre* sufficed for a whole month. But Hedvig would not touch it.

"Good enough for that young humbug, yes."

Once more Egholm felt his hands itching with murderous instincts, but when the tension was at its height, a spark flew over to some nerve of humour. He bent down almost double, put one hand to his mouth like a funnel, and whispered in his wife's ear:

"Sh! Remember, his father's an Angel!"

The Evangelist closed his puffy eyes reflectively for a moment when Egholm returned and stated what was the menu for the day.

"H'm. I'll stay, all the same," he said. And added a moment after: "If there's eggs, I like them hard boiled."

"Hard boiled—yes, yes," said Egholm, precisely in the manner of a waiter, and disappeared into the kitchen once more.

"I never heard the like—that rascally scamp ... thinks we can dig up eggs out of the ground—and that in December! Why, only to ask at the grocer's they'd think we were mad. Eggs, indeed! *Eggs—on credit!* No, as long as we can get what's barely needful. Why...."

But Egholm, with great ends in view, wasted little time in talk. He went out himself, and returned five minutes later with a bag of eggs and a lump of sausage, which he set down triumphantly on the kitchen table. Thus supper was provided of a kind to exceed Karlsen's expectations, and set him in good humour.

Both laughed, Karlsen, however, the louder, when the host's egg was found to be bad. As for the clove tea, Karlsen, like Hedvig, did not find it to his taste. He explained that he liked something with a little more colour, his taste and smell having suffered through smoking.

Then, at a suitable moment, Egholm said:

"My wife says she won't come into the Brotherhood at any price—not just at the moment, that is to say. But perhaps later, I've no doubt ... that is to say...."

And he waited for the answer with the sweat standing out on his forehead.

"Oh, well, never mind. Hang the condition. We'll leave it out."

Egholm could have knelt at his feet.

Karlsen went on to tell of the Brotherhood and its doings. Everything was going on first-rate. Fru Westergaard had got dropsy, and there was every likelihood—here Karlsen clicked his tongue in anticipation—every likelihood of her bequeathing them a whole heap of money. The Angel went to see her practically every day, and, in case of need, the Prophet from Copenhagen would come too.

"Father's in touch with a heap of them, you know. By letter. He got a letter the other day from John the Apostle. He's in London."

"John the Apostle? You don't mean.... Is that...."

"Exactly. He lives in London. Don't you know it's written: 'If he tarry till I come, what is that to thee?' Yes, he'll be here all right, up to the day of the coming again. Father's got his address, but he keeps himself quiet, you understand, mostly. And Father doesn't say where he is, but I managed to get hold of it, all the same. I sent him a picture post card from Veile only yesterday."

Egholm ran in to borrow a pipe from Marinus. On the way he whispered to his wife:

"He's the biggest liar on earth. But if only he'd hand over that money.... I can't stand the suspense. Put in a prayer meanwhile."

The Evangelist puffed great clouds, and delivered another turn or so.

"I've something to tell you, my dear friend—in confidence, that is. *The Star of Bethlehem's been seen!*"

He bent over Egholm and stared full into his eyes.

"Yes, the Star of Bethlehem—right over Odense, it was."

And he puffed a spurt of smoke into Egholm's face, his own contracting into an unconcealed grin.

"My father, the Angel, was standing in his office, and he saw it. It isn't everyone that can see it, you know. But I could. It was the hugest star I've ever seen."

Egholm condescended to shake his head as if deeply impressed. For the rest, his every nerve-cell was concentrating in an effort to hypnotise Karlsen's hand into Karlsen's pocket for that bundle of notes.

At eleven minutes past seven the Evangelist laid down his pipe and buttoned his coat.

"The money! Er—you'll excuse me, but—you're not forgetting ... that gift.... No hurry, of course, not in the least...."

"You shall have it. I'm not forgetting it, no," said Karlsen, with unction. "It's not a great sum, but with the blessing of the Lord it may go a long way."

He drew out a leather purse with a string from his pocket, unfastened the lace with exasperating care, and flung out a hand with a two-*kroner* piece.

"Two *kroner*! Is that—the gift? Karlsen, you don't mean it!" said Egholm, weeping.

"One *daler*, yes," said Karlsen, laughing heartily. But his expression changed suddenly, possibly influenced by Egholm's threatening look, and, resuming his dignified manner, he went on:

"The gift was originally forty-two *kroner* altogether, that being the sum found when the box was opened. Fru Westergaard gave thirty-five herself. You were in her good books, my friend."

Karlsen allowed himself a momentary lapse from dignity to the extent of a single wink.

"The rocking-chair," murmured Egholm reminiscently.

"But," went on the Evangelist, "you owed arrears of tithe ever since February of last year...."

His voice grew thick with imminent laughter.

"So we decided to annex the forty *kroner* for tithes—and here's the rest!"

"Decided ... who decided? When the money was collected for me? Impossible!"

"The congregation agreed to it," said Karlsen unconcernedly. Then suddenly he dug one thumb into his despairing brother's ribs, uttered a sound like the rasp of a saw, and whispered:

"And Fru Westergaard was there, too—my son!"

Limp and utterly dispirited, Egholm walked up with Karlsen to the station. A strange feeling of detachment had come over him, and the inclination to weep that he always felt after great excitement.

Karlsen walked a couple of paces ahead, talking gaily over his shoulder.

"What say?" queried Egholm against the wind. The handbag with edifying works at six *kroner* cloth boards weighed heavily in his numbed hand.

"I say, it's a good thing we're near the end of the month."

"Yes," agreed Egholm. "But what d'you mean?"

"Pay day, my dear man. And I can do with it!"

"But I thought—I thought the work was voluntary. It says in the Rules of the Brotherhood...."

"Well, what d'you expect me to live on?"

"Why, gifts."

"Huh! A long way that'd go. About as far as...."

"No, of course...." agreed Egholm meekly, shifting the bag to his other hand.

"But they don't pay me enough," said the Evangelist harshly. "Not by a long way. Everything's getting dearer, and I've had a lot of extra expenses into the bargain. I helped a poor girl that had got into trouble. A Frøken Madsen. Bought her a cigar shop in Kerteminde; it cost an awful sum. But she was a sort of relation—not of mine, you understand. My wife's people. But I count it all the same, of course. No, they'll have to give me a rise. And they will, too, I know. They can't do without me, and that's the end of it."

They reached the station, and Karlsen took his ticket.

"*Second* class, I said," he cried, and winked at Egholm.

"Came from Veile, and going back to Veile. Life's one long journey. Anyhow, it's what we're supposed to do: go out into the world and make converts. Know a man named Justesen in Veile? Horse-dealer. No? Ah, he's a man if you like! Never troubles to ask the price when he finds a pair to suit him. 'Bring 'em along'—that's all he says."

"Horse-dealers don't go in much for religion as a rule."

"Not him—no. But his wife!" said Karlsen, rasping again like a saw. "His wife.... Had a wire from Justesen last evening; he's coming home to-day and going off again by the night train to Hamburg. So off I go to look up my old friend Egholm—what?"

"Yes...." said Egholm.

He stood in the waiting-room a little after the train had gone, warming himself by the stove. Then he shook his head and staggered off homewards.

Again and again he tried to reckon up how he stood.

"No hope of getting to work on the boat now," he muttered. But, to his surprise, he found his thoughts refused to dwell on this disaster, which should by rights have overshadowed all else.

No; he could think of one thing—he was hungry.

For months past he had not had a decent meal, and, though he had not realised it himself, his looking forward to that gift from the Brotherhood had been associated with an indomitable desire for *food*.

Outside his own door he stopped. The scent of the clove tea came to greet him, and revolted him for the first time. He turned round and walked away again, out over the sandhills, along the quay, and down between the warehouses.

The group of fishermen sighted his thin, fluttering figure in the gloom, shook themselves, and pressed their backs closer against the wall of the shed.

But Egholm found at last an old green rowing boat among those drawn up on the beach. He struck a match, and made sure it was the one.

Then he clambered up on to it, and knelt down on the boards.

The wind tore his plaintive prayer to shreds, and strewed a shower of broken, unmeaning sounds out over the harbour and the town.

XVIII

Egholm's God was perhaps not as generous as might be wished, but, on the other hand, possessed of limitless patience as a listener, differing in this regard considerably from the children of men. It was perhaps this which led Egholm, the ever restless, to come again faithfully with his hopes and his prayers, though he might have turned away in dudgeon but a short while back.

It was not brain-weariness. That was an ailment Egholm never knew. He lived, as it were, under full sail all day and night. He rose in the morning, swallowed his clove tea, hurried out to his place of prayer in the woods, and came back about dinner-time. Then he would mess about for a few hours in the studio, while his thoughts flew all ways at will, generally down to the beach, where he struggled with imaginary parts of his machine in an imaginary boat, but ready and willing to occupy themselves with anything of any sort anywhere in the world. Egholm felt it a wasted day when he had not stowed away a couple of new inventions in the warehouse of his mind. And a night that brought him nothing but sleep and rest he counted empty and unfruitful. Better a touch of the horrors than just nothing. For, painful as it was to have Clara Steen's face there before him in the dark, taking the blows that Anna should have had, still, after all—in the long run—one could get used to anything. Yes.

True, it was no use striking Anna, but it was at least excusable. And God never said anything about it to him out in the woods where he prayed. More especially since that boy had come home it was excusable … nay, it was a simple necessity.

Thus Egholm forgave his God and revenged himself on his family.

His wife noticed, too, how the boy's coming had brought a kind of ferment into their home life. Ah, why should it be so? There he sat, the little lad, at her side, as simple and innocent as when he was a child, helping her at her work. She did all she could to make him appear a harmless and useful item about the house. She would have liked to make him invisible, but his father *saw* the boy to the exclusion of all else, circled round him, shot sparks at him, and might be found gripping him by the hair if she only went out into the kitchen for a minute.

Things could not go on like this. And so one afternoon she put on the best things she possessed, and went out with Sivert to try and find him a place.

With trembling knees she walked straight into Lund's smart drapery shop. After all, he couldn't do more than eat her. And she always went to him for what she needed in the way of thread and material, and that was the truth. They stood just inside the door, waiting for other customers to be served first. Modesty, that was the way.

There! Minna Lund, the daughter of the house, coming in with coffee for the assistant. Was there ever such a place? She set down the tray on a stepladder, and began pulling out drawers full of ribbons.

A little princess, that was the least one could call her—though little was hardly the word, seeing she was half a head taller than her father. Why, she could wind off as many yards of ribbon as she pleased, without even asking the price.

And the mother, standing there, fell to weaving a long and beautiful future for her boy in Lund's splendid house. Those two young people—they would surely have an eye to each other…. And then when Sivert's apprenticeship was at an end, and Lund was getting on in years, who knows…. Once they found out what a heart the boy had, surely there'd be no one in the world they'd sooner trust with their daughter and the shop….

She pressed Sivert's hand; for here was Lund himself right in front of her, bowing politely. He wouldn't eat her, no fear of that….

So Fru Egholm had thought of having her son apprenticed to the business? Why, a nice idea, to be sure….

Lund was a little man with a full beard, and elegantly dressed in brand-new things, but with a thread or a piece of fluff here and there. And his manner was precisely the same.

He talked with studied ease and distinction, flourishing the roll of material before him into a fan as he spoke. And so thoroughly did he possess the gift of salesmanship that a moment later Fru Egholm was eagerly discussing with him how much it would take for a pair of curtains.

"Or we've a rather better quality," said Lund, reaching for another roll. But here Fru Egholm came to herself, and thrust Sivert forward.

"Well, you know, I'm afraid," said Lund kindly—he had only forgotten the business of the apprenticeship for a moment—"we could hardly … you see, we make a point of taking only boys—pupils in the business that is—from better-class homes. The customers demand it."

"But"—the mother was ready to sink into the ground for shame—but … Sivert *was* from a better-class home. Not meaning herself, of course, but her husband. He knew all sorts of languages, English and French and so on. And only a little time back he'd been an assistant on the railway—why they had his uniform coat in the house now! Hr. Lund ought just to hear him talk and speak up for himself, like he did with those people from the Public Health Committee. And as for Sivert, he was as good and honest a lad as any could wish to have.

Hr. Lund didn't doubt it for a moment, but—er—well, one could hardly see it, for instance, from the way he was dressed, you know. Now, could you? And Lund bent over the counter with a smile, whereby his own coat was brought in close proximity to Sivert's blouse. He he! Still, he might just examine the young man a little. Sivert was given two or three smart questions, while his mother was on the point of swooning from confusion. Then Lund turned calmly round and took down the roll of material before mentioned—the rather better quality....

"But how about the place?" asked Fru Egholm doubtfully. "Is he to have it?"

"Eh? Oh, no. I've no use for him. Did you notice he said 'drawers'? Well, 'knickers' is the proper word—at any rate, the one we use in this establishment. A little trap of mine, you know. He he!"

Fru Egholm sighed, purchased resignedly a reel of No. 50 white, and left the shop. She and Sivert went to many places that day—to a barber's, to Bro, the grocer, and at last to the editor of the *Knarreby News*—only to wander home at last discouraged at a total failure all round.

Well, she would leave it for a day or two, and look round.

"Find him a place?" asked Egholm.

"Well—there's places enough where they'd be glad to have him...."

"That is to say, you *didn't* find him a place?"

Fru Egholm was so very loth to utter that little decisive "No." She talked eagerly about the Christmas sales at Bro's and Lund's.

"... And, do you know, the editor, he knew about your plans with the machine business. He asked a heap of things, and said you were a genius."

The subject was wisely chosen. And it did draw off attention for the moment from the matter in hand, but then her husband lapsed into his gloomy thoughts once more.

"No—we'll never get rid of him now. Who'd ever have him? What can you use a head like that for, anyway? He's little better than a lunatic. Eh? What do you say?"

Here Fru Egholm suddenly appeared unwontedly versed in the Scriptures. She answered boldly, and with emphasis:

"Well, there's one place where Sivert won't be set behind the rest—even if they're ever so much of a genius."

"Eh, what—what do you say?"

"I say: *Blessed are the poor in spirit, for theirs is the Kingdom of Heaven!*"

Egholm gasped, utterly at a loss, and made no answer.

Sivert slept in the little back room where Hedvig had her couch. He lay on the floor, upon a sort of bed of some nondescript material, and slept in his clothes to keep warm. Nevertheless, he went to bed with a smile on his lips. His father's persecution could not shatter his joy at being *at home*. Even the blows and kicks he got beat into him the fact that he was at home, and he took them without complaint. Yes, all was well, everything.

Next morning, as Egholm was gulping down his tea, he caught sight of Sivert's bowed and huddled figure slipping across the yard. Ordinarily, Sivert stole out of his room by the window, and kept out of the way till his father had gone out—there was no sense in giving him the trouble of getting angry if it could be avoided. But to-day the boy had overslept himself.

Egholm reached out and rapped at the window, at the imminent risk of breaking the glass.

Sivert stopped, gave a sickly smile, turned round twice where he stood, and made towards the gate.

"Here, you fool!" roared his father, and Sivert stopped again.

"Be quick and come in," whispered his mother out from the kitchen door.

"Well, why don't you come? Put on your cap and come along with me."

Sivert obeyed without a word.

Egholm held the boy close to his side, and they marched down the path towards the beach.

"Go on ahead, so I can keep an eye on you," he commands. And Sivert walks on ahead with the transcendent smile of the martyr-about-to-be. He knows now he is to die, but it doesn't matter so much, after all. Going to drown him, he supposes, since they are making towards the water.

"Know what you've got to do?" asks his father.

"Yes," says Sivert, smiling again. And a little after, he ventures to add: "But if—if you don't mind, I'd like it better if you'd take a nice soft stone and batter my head with it. I'd die quite soon that way...."

"Soft stone?" says Egholm mechanically, busy with his own thoughts. "Nonsense. You walk straight on; that's all you've got to do."

"Ah well," sighs Sivert, breaking into a trot. "I was only thinking, perhaps I'm not a good one to drown, after all. I can't swim, you know."

"Who's talking about drowning? That can wait till to-morrow, anyway. You're coming out with me to a place of mine, to pray."

"I think I'd like that better, yes," said Sivert. But his voice showed only the slightest possible change of tone.

They walked along the beach a long way, out to the woods. Sivert walked with an unsteady gait; he would really rather have died after all if only he might be left to himself for a single minute first.... But his father drove him on like a donkey in front. The boy's strangeness of manner irritated him.

"Walk properly, boy, and keep your mind on godly things!"

"Yes," said Sivert, and managed to call to mind a verse of a hymn, which he proceeded to mutter as he went. But he still walked unsteadily, bending spasmodically every now and then.

"We can stop here," said his father, as they reached a wooded slope, where some young pines stood out from a thin covering of snow.

"Do you know the text: 'Blessed are the poor in spirit'? Good. We'll say that text, and then a prayer, that you'll repeat after me word for word. You understand?"

Then, while they were still in the preparatory stage, kneeling opposite each other with bared heads, something happened which destroyed at one blow all possibility of further co-operation.

Under cover of his cap, held before him in his folded hands, Sivert has managed to undo one button....

Egholm hears a peculiar sound ... springs up with a roar....

Off goes Sivert like a hare across the ice, unable to stop what he had already begun. It looked as if he were spinning a thread behind him like a spider. He had no intention of returning, however. He had but one thought—home.

Egholm did not attempt to pursue. He tried to go on with his prayer, but gave it up, and went into the woods. He walked all the morning, and came round by a wide detour into Knarreby about dinner-time. But his haste was such that he passed by the house without thought of hunger or thirst. Not till he was in the main street did he slacken his pace, and begin looking absently into the shop windows. They were crammed with all manner of things—Christmas was near. There were ducks, and these he noticed in particular, but all the rest made one confused medley to his eyes. Nevertheless, he went up to the next window and gazed at it attentively, as if mentally selecting something specially rare and costly as a present for his love.

Then, at the sale department of the ironfoundry, he came to himself again. Here at last were things worth looking at. Right up against the glass were lovely heavy castings, pieces of machinery, and metal parts. Pumps of all sizes, stacks of copper and brass tubing, taps and boiler gauges, and heaps of nuts and bolts and screws, as if a wagon load had been tipped down at random. Then there were spiral coils of the most delicious lead and hempen packing, and farther back, at the end of the shop, stood a mail-clad army of stoves. Somehow or other, Egholm always found comfort in the sight of masses of cold metal. Possibly it drew off the warmth of his over-heated brain.

Rothe, the ironfounder, a giant of a man, stood on the steps calling to passers-by in greeting: "*Goddag, goddag!*"—the words seemed to echo in the shield-like cavity of his stomach. His great head shone as if it were of burnished copper. Now he caught sight of Egholm.

"Hey, *goddag, goddag*, Egholm! How's the turbine getting on?"

Egholm walked in and spluttered out his latest ideas. Rothe laughed, and slapped him genially on the shoulder.

"Henrik Vang's full of it. Talks of nothing else down at the hotel. But, look here—when are you going to get it *done*? Egholm's famous turbine...."

"Well, there's one or two little things I still want," said Egholm, walking round the shop and fingering the items that caught his attention.

"What sort of things?"

"A boat, for instance, and a small boiler." Egholm mentioned these as carelessly as if it had been a matter of a couple of waistcoat buttons. "But"—he broke off suddenly—"what's that thing there?" He dragged at something in the warehouse behind.

"That? Oh, that's Dr. Hoff's old bath oven. I've just sent him a new one."

Egholm was still pulling the thing about, when Rothe, who was in his best lunch-time and Christmas-time mood, said:

"If it's any good to you, bring round a barrow and take it along."

Whereupon he slapped Egholm again on the shoulder, and took up his post again at the door, dealing out his double-barrelled greetings: "*Goddag—goddag!*"

Egholm was in high spirits for quite a time over his unexpected coup. Then, happening to catch sight of himself in a mirror-backed window, he started in horror to see what a ghastly figure he made.

Yellow and haggard, with his black beard hanging limp and dead over his worn and stained waistcoat. A disgusting sight.

Could it really be the Lord's intention to starve him to death?

The thought almost brought him to his knees; he turned in through the churchyard gate, as to a refuge where he could recover himself. The naked branches of the mighty chestnuts sang in the wind, and great heavy drops fell like tears from the roof of the church.

The wind must have changed. It was thawing now.

Egholm noticed that he no longer felt the biting cold. Perhaps, after all, it was not so cruelly meant.

One end of the fire-ladder had fallen down. Egholm seated himself on it, with his back against the church wall. He was physically exhausted, and his brain had hardly rested for the past twenty-four hours.

It generally made him feel better to come in here for a while and look out over the landscape he loved.

There at his feet lay the Custom House, its acute-angled roof just on a level with the church foundations. Down in the office there sat Old Poulsen at one window and Wassermann himself at the other. Funny thing, really, that Poulsen should be called Old Poulsen, for the sake of the few grey hairs about his ears—he was an infant, really, compared with Wassermann.

How old could Wassermann be? Some said eighty-eight, but, looking at his mummy-face, one might feel more inclined to think he had stood as a man in the prime of life, wearing his gold-braided cap, what time Noah's Ark had landed on Mount Ararat, and he had come to examine the ship's papers.

Egholm gave a little grunt.

There was but a single vessel in the harbour—a schooner, laid up for the winter. Its masts looked thin and, as it were, leafless, with the sails and rigging taken down. The boys had built themselves a snow hut out on the ice under its bowsprit. The current of the Belt was too strong just here for the ice to hold it altogether in check; a little farther north, there had been a battle between the two, and the ice had lost. Mighty sheets of it came floating down the channel; off the mole, they packed and closed in an angry whirl, setting their teeth in the piles, but were torn away ruthlessly and sent on southward again.

In the curve of the channel between the black woods, the ice-floes looked like a flock of white swans on a blue lake. The grey-green line of hills on the Jutland side looked far away in the misty air, though the distance was not so great but that one could count the windows of the ferry station over between the trees.

Egholm's brain had rested for just the space of time it took to turn his head from right to left and back again. Now it began hammering again; he had caught sight of a certain green-painted dinghy down by the harbour, and that particular craft interested him more than all the other rowing boats in the world.

But—in Heaven's name—how was he to gain possession?

He rose, and went down into the coal-cellar of the church, where he commenced to pray. His thoughts were confused with excitement, he did not understand his own words, and when he stood up again, the coals came rattling down with a sound as of scornful laughter. Could a man go to the devil and get hold of fifty *kroner* that way?

Or, could not a man settle the business himself, by his own unaided power? Why this constant begging round?

Egholm walked out of the churchyard, talking to himself, and took the road to Kongeskoven—thus completing the whole circuit of the town and neighbourhood for that day.

All his inventions, were they of no more value when it came to the point than that he must die of hunger? Surely there should be some appreciation of them—at any rate, in higher quarters. He thought of some of the more important; not mere ideas he had busied himself with to pass the time, shaking them out of his sleeve like a conjurer, but those that were really worth something, say, a million.

As, for instance, the pair of frictionless wheels for railway carriages—that should have meant an income to the inventor out of every pair of wheels in all the world, if only God had lifted a little finger to help.

And then that preparation of his for turning yellow bricks red—a profit of several *kroner* per thousand of bricks!

There was Egholm's smoke-consumer, that would make the atmosphere of great cities as pure as the purest sea air.

There was ... but, no; it was enough. These three supreme inventions of his were in themselves sufficient to condemn that God up there!

Plainly, God was not disposed to help: He kept down genius out of sheer envy.

Egholm walked into the woods, beating his breast and threatening high Heaven. Once he happened to strike himself on the mouth, and this set his thoughts off in an entirely new direction, where they tore away even more furiously, and flung themselves cascading into headlong depths.

The blow had reminded him of that last affair with Anna—yesterday morning, was it, or the day before?

"It's a lie!" he hissed, kicking at a root. "A downright lie, fostered in a venomous woman's brain. Her nose came on to bleed, that was all. Just an ordinary case of nose-bleeding, that happened to come on at the same time. But, of course, she made the most of it. I didn't do anything worse than"—here he lashed out with his stick—"other days, but then she starts screaming hysterically, and there's the blood trickling down through her fingers. Ugly—horrible...."

What was that?

Egholm came to a standstill in the middle of the path, and looked round with staring eyes.

What was this? Was he to be haunted now, in broad daylight? Surely it might at least have the decency to wait till night?

No; it was here. The same old story from his sleepless nights; the fights with Anna over again. Every word that had been spoken between them. And then, at the decisive moment—the loved and detested face of Clara Steen rising up to take the blows—Clara's white fingers vainly trying to stop that crimson stream.... Clara's eyes, looking at him....

"I must be ill, I think," he murmured to himself. "And there's a nasty pain here in the middle of my chest. Throbbing and throbbing like anything. Not quite in the middle, though—no, a little to the left."

He burst out into a wild laugh and beat his forehead with the back of his hand.

Not so strange, after all, that it should be more to the left. The heart was on the left side. Ha ha! yes, he was a witty fellow, after all!

But the drama was still going on before his eyes. Oh, but he would not see it. No, no—not here in the daytime. For the love of God, let the curtain fall! Leave it till the night, when all sorts of things happened anyway, beyond understanding. Here, in the middle of the road, he could not go smashing pictures in broad daylight. It was too much to ask.

And—well, he was ready to admit, if that would help at all, that it wasn't just ordinary nose-bleeding. No, Heaven help him, he had struck her with all his force right across nose and mouth. Well, then, now he had confessed. Wasn't that enough?

Where was the sense of being an inventor and a natural healer, if he could not find a pain-killer for his own case?

Still, perhaps he might, after all. Suppose, now, he were to make one smart cut and tear that beating heart right out, all would be well.

Next moment he sawed the fancy across with a grin. Ugh! poetic nonsense!

No—but there was something else—something far better....

Here, close by, must be Fruedammen, the Lady Pool, where a noble dame had once disappeared in her bridal chariot with all eight horses. Surely it would make things easier to get down deep into that?

Aha! Good old inventor—never at a loss!

He hung his stick over his arm and folded his hands.

"Forgive me, Heavenly Father, for this once—for just this once."

Some critical self within himself marked the words as lisping and ridiculous.

He ran at a stumbling trot along the ground over the serpentine contortions of the great beech roots. It could not be more than a minute's walk to the pool. But there was no time to be lost.

Curious, by the way, that a man should for close on fifty years have clung to life tooth and nail, and now, to-day, on Christmas Eve, be hurrying to get rid of it.

What would they say to it all at home?

Would Hedvig stand up straight and stiff and say, "A good thing, too"?

And Emanuel, the child of victory, what would be his future? Ah, well, there was little victory to be expected there, after all. No, that turbine was the true victory child.

Farewell, smooth round thing, that should have gone one day with a soft "dut-dut," while all the world shouted hurrah and wept at the same moment.

Egholm found himself weeping at the thought, and his legs grew weak under him, but he kept up his pace, and took a last evasive mental farewell of Anna as he went.

Now, just across to the other side of the road—here it was.

There was a little low seat with many initials cut in. Egholm ran round it, swept past a thorn-bush, tearing his face against the branches, and stood breathing heavily on the brink of the bottomless pool in the forest.

A chill shudder passed through him. His head sank forward. A moment after he gave a queer little laugh, shrugged his shoulders, then staggered up to a tree and leaned against it.

On the farther side of the pool, a blackbird was rustling in the leaves; now it flew off with a long whistling cry. It was a little past noon. Now and again a draggled ray of sunlight slipped through the covering of clouds, and the branches threw pale shadows in its gleam. Only a second they remained, then vanished again like spirits.

Egholm felt his knees sinking—he was deadly tired. Then, at the sound of a cart crushing through the wood far away, he drew himself up with a sigh and walked off among the trees.

The blood began pulsing in long swells through his veins, following on his excitement, but there was no pain anywhere now. He had a nice strong feeling of having been honest.

He murmured a few words of Sivert's oracular speech that had stuck in his mind:

"It's ever so hard to do a thing when it's impossible."

Suppose he tried laughing a little at the whole thing. He had hurried to the pool—and lo, the ice was Heaven knows how many inches thick. Of course, it was. Still, he had been honest—God was his witness to that. It must have been the open water of the Belt that made him forget.

It was evening before he found himself back, wiping his shoes carefully and gently in the passage. So unwontedly gentle was he, indeed, that Anna came out in a fright with the lamp to see who was there.

"Oh, heavens, is it you, Egholm? We've been almost out of our wits because you didn't come back. Wherever have you been all day?"

She rubbed his wet things with a towel, and told of the joint of pork that had come from the Christmas Charity Committee, and the cakes that Hedvig had brought home.

She rubbed away, chattering all the time, mentioning casually what a blessing it was Sivert had got that place with the glazier's—to have his own room and all. She stopped, astounded at her own boldness in daring to utter Sivert's name.

But Egholm made no sound, and she went on, scraping the mud from his boots the while, to tell how she had just happened to think of Nøckel, the glazier, if he might happen to want a boy, and she had hardly got inside the door when they said yes, and were glad to have him.

"He can stay here this evening—if you like," said his father.

Fru Egholm could hardly believe her ears, and Sivert, carefully hidden away in the pantry, fancied, too, that there must be something queer behind it all.

"Don't somehow feel like being thrashed to-day, either," he said, darkly reflecting.

So the Egholms had some sort of a Christmas, after all. The gentler feelings flourished in every heart. Egholm himself gave orders that Marinus from the carpenter's shop should be sent for, having found him gazing longingly in through a window. On Christmas Eve, it was a duty to entertain the poor at one's table, he said, if one wanted to feel any Christmas rejoicing oneself. His wife found this a very pretty sentiment, with the one reservation that the principle, to her mind, was followed out to an extreme degree in their case, since the five who were daily entertained at their board were undeniably poor themselves.

Later in the evening, she went to the window, and with a certain awkwardness brought over the champagne blossom and set it on a chair in the middle of the room with a candle in front. Anyone could see it was meant to be a Christmas tree, all ready decked. Marinus giggled at Sivert, but Hedvig rose of her own accord, stepped out into their midst like an actress, and sang till the windows rattled about sweet and joyous Christmastide.

"Now we ought to hand round the presents," said Fru Egholm to Marinus, with a laugh.

Egholm joined absently in the laugh. He had a vague idea of having already received a Christmas present that was worth something.

He had been given back his life.

And that was, after all, a thing of some importance, if he was ever to get that turbine done.

XIX

After a cruel winter came the spring at last, offering gentle hands to all mankind. Folk might be seen walking in the streets, hat in hand, in gratitude and veneration towards the bright, happy face of the sun.

It was much the same with the flowers; they came forth in hosts from out of the earth, *saw* the sun, and bowed.

The beech, knowing its flowers were nothing to speak of, put on its pale green silk first thing in the morning, and found no reason to be ashamed, but the apple tree surpassed them all; it had to put on its bridal dress with a blush.

Fru Egholm left the kitchen window open all day long. A branch from Andreasen's espalier, an apple branch of all things, thrust itself up across the opening. It was almost her property, so to speak, that apple branch. She showed Emanuel how the bees came flying up, whispered something sweet into the ears of the little flower things, and were given honeyed kisses in return before flying off again.

Fru Egholm did more than that for her little boy; she got Hedvig to take him out every afternoon into the meadow near by. He came home with a chain of dandelion stalks round his neck, and one day he even had a dead butterfly in his clammy little fist. That day, he could hardly speak for the wonders he had seen.

Spring came to Egholm, too. He had got his boat—the very green one he had prayed for. Vang had procured it for him, by some means unknown.

"My dear fellow, my old and trusted friend, let me make you a present of it. Here you are, the boat is yours, presented by a circle of friends."

And the pair overflowed in a transport of mutual affection.

The boiler was already in its place, and the funnel towered proudly above, painted a fine bold red. The screw stuck out behind, and could revolve when turned by hand. All looked well, so far.

But the turbine itself, the beating heart that was to make the thing alive, was not yet finished.

Krogh, the old blacksmith, worked away at it till his yellow drooping jaws shook. His tools were mediæval. What a machine drill could have managed in an afternoon, he took a week to do. Egholm turned up his eyes to heaven, when he saw how little had been done in twenty-four hours, but he said nothing. The fact was, that Krogh had one quality which rendered him more valuable than all other blacksmiths together: he was willing to work without seeing the money first. Moreover, his work was good when it *was* done, and in spite of his sour looks, he took a real interest in the project.

Egholm was so kindly and easy to get on with all that spring that his wife was quite uneasy about him at times. All the hours he could spare from his studio—and they, alas, were not a few—he spent down on the beach, scraping and patching and painting his wonderful creation.

At home, he would sit dreaming in the arm-chair, so far removed from all reality that Emanuel might sing and prattle as much as he pleased without being stopped by a peremptory order from his father.

He was sitting thus one evening towards the end of May; both Emanuel and Hedvig were asleep. The day had been hot, and the heat still hung in the low-ceiled rooms. The children were tossing restlessly in their beds. If only one dared to open a window—but no; the night air was a thing to be careful about, while there were children in the place, thought Fru Egholm to herself. It was late, very late, but what did that matter, as long as there was oil enough in the lamp?

"Whatever are you sitting there thinking about?" she asked, when the silence had lasted an eternity. There was not the slightest danger now in such a piece of familiarity on her part. Not as he had been lately.

"Nothing," said Egholm, drawing in his breath as if he had just emerged from the depths of the sea. "What's that you're fussing about now?"

"Wassermann's wig. Look at it—it's simply falling to pieces. But as for a new one—well, you should have seen his wife's face when I spoke of it. And if it hadn't been that there's a chance they might take Hedvig as maid there, I'd never...."

"What d'you get for a bit of work like that?"

"Well, it ought to be a *krone*, but seventy-five *øre* I will have, and that's the least. Though I don't suppose she'll offer me more than fifty, the stingy old wretch."

Egholm sat silent a while, then involuntarily he lied a little. "I'll tell you," he said, "what I was thinking about. You know that verse from '*Adam Homo*':

> "'What trouble's worst? We've trials enough, Lord knows
> If I should ask, a score of voices swift
> Would tell me where *they* found the "little rift"
> Each as experience led him to suppose.

> One says 'tis boredom, one, 'tis married life;
> Another finds it worse *without* a wife.
> One thinks remorsefully of sins committed,
> Another with regret of those omitted.
> One, of all pains we've suffered since the Fall,
> Will reckon *Money Troubles* worst of all.'

Yes, money troubles—that's the worst. Paludan Müller, he knew. And he's my favourite poet. He knew everything!"

And Egholm fell to talking pitifully of poverty, the nightmare that had its teeth in his throat, and could not be torn away.

"But there's more comes after," said Anna, when he paused. "Don't you remember the next verse?"

"I know the whole thing off by heart. Anywhere you like to choose."

"Well, then, you know that money troubles aren't the worst in the world. It's no good losing courage like that. And we're getting on nicely now, really. Etatsraaden said about the rhubarb, we might…."

She put forth all her womanly arts to comfort him, but in vain. Still she kept on—and her voice was much the same as when she was soothing Emanuel.

Egholm let her go on; yes, they were getting on nicely now, he thought to himself, and smiled bitterly. Oh yes, nicely, magnificently!

The globe of the lamp was stuck together with strips of newspaper. Before the window hung a piece of faded green stuff in two tapes, drooping down to a slack fold in the middle. At the sides were ragged, dusty curtains, into which Anna had stuck some paper flowers.

On the walls were a couple of old engravings, an embroidered newspaper-holder of his wife's, and a few fretwork brackets and photograph frames, these being Sivert's work.

The big mirror, too, looked ridiculous, really, at that angle—it had to be slanted forward to an excessive degree, owing to the lowness of the room. Egholm could see himself in it, and the children's bed as well. Emanuel lay on the settee, but Hedvig's bed, in the little side room, consisted of three chairs. Her coverlet was his old uniform cloak, and the chairs rocked at every breath she drew.

Poverty in every corner. The very pattern of the wallpaper was formed of holes and patches of damp.

True, there were the two arm-chairs and the chest of drawers, but….

His wife was still talking away of all the good things they had to be thankful for. Of Hedvig, coming home regularly with her good wages, and the chance now of getting a place at ten *kroner*, at Wassermann's. And then Sivert, still at the glazier's this ever so long. Surely it was a mercy they could be proud of their children?

And soon Egholm himself would have finished that steamboat thing of his…. Fru Egholm threw out this last by some chance, having exhausted all other items that could reasonably be included.

Her husband started. It was what he had been thinking of all the evening himself. But, anxious not to betray the fact, he said only:

"Yes; if I'm lucky."

But Anna saw through him all the same. Stupid of her not to have thought before of the one thing that was all the world to him.

"And why shouldn't you be lucky, I should like to know? You haven't lost faith in your own invention?"

"It's a curious thing," he said, leaning back in his chair. "One moment I believe in it, and the next I don't. How is it possible that the trained experts with all modern equipment at their backs—and money, most of all—with nothing to worry about but their own calculations and plans—how could they have missed the solution of the problem when it seems to me as plain as the nose on your face?"

"Why, as to that, I don't know, I'm sure. But that steam cart you made, you know, just before Hedvig was born, that didn't work."

"Oh, what's that got to do with it?" said Egholm irritably.

His wife pointed warningly towards the sleeping children. "Sh!" she said. Then, noticing that the cloak had slipped down from Hedvig's legs, she hastened to tuck it up again. Egholm calmed down.

"Don't mix up a steam cart and a turbine," he said when she re-entered the room. "I didn't take any particular trouble over that steam cart—at any rate, not enough. After all, it was only construction work, that. But a turbine that can *reverse*—that's an independent invention. I'd give my heart's blood to realise it. You know what a friction coupling is, I suppose?"

"Do you mean the thing with the two balls, that swing round and look like an umbrella?"

"Good heavens, no! You're thinking of a centrifugal regulator valve."

"Oh well, well, then…."

No, it was no use talking to her; she muddled up the simplest things imaginable. Egholm wrung his hands and was silent.

But a little after, he looked up brightly and suggested they should go and have a look at the machinery now, both together.

Anna shook her head. What an idea!

"Aren't you a bit interested in my things?"

"Why, that you know I am, Egholm. But you wouldn't ask me to go running out now in the middle of the night. Look, it's half-past one!"

"But you say you never can go out in the daytime."

This was true; Anna never set foot outside the door as long as it was light. Her dress had been ruined altogether this winter, from having to use it for Emanuel's bedclothes at night. And what was the use of having rooms across a courtyard, when Andreasen's workmen came running to the window every time they heard the door?

"But the lamp might upset, and the house burn down and the children in it."

"Turn it out, then, of course. Don't talk such a lot."

Fru Egholm writhed; there was no persuading him any way once he had taken a thing into his head.

Hesitatingly she took out a white knitted kerchief from a drawer. She had almost forgotten what it was like to put on one's things to go out....

It was moonlight outside; the shadow of the tall workshop roof lay coal-black over half the courtyard, leaving the remainder white as if it had been lime-washed.

Every step she took seemed new and strange. So softly their steps fell in the thick dust as they crossed the road.

Up in the old churchyard, every tree stood like a temple of perfume in the quiet, soft night. And all the time, she was marvelling that it really *was* moonlight. She had not noticed it at home—doubtless because the lamp was burning.

The tears came into her eyes—just such a moonlight night it had been the time they....

And here she was walking with him, just as then.

Surely, it was enough to turn one's head.

Here was Egholm actually taking her arm. Taking her arm!...

Great moths and small glided silently past; one of them vanished into the hedge as if by magic.

Bats showed up here and there against the pale sky, flung about like leaves in the wind. From the meadow came a quivering chorus of a thousand frogs.

"It must be like this in Paradise," she said faintly.

"Ah, wait till you can see the boat," said her husband.

The dew on the thick grass down by the beach soaked through her boots and stockings. Moonlight *and* stockings wet with dew.... Oh, it was not *just like* that time now; it *was* that time ... that night at Aalborg, after the dance at the assembly rooms, where she had met the interesting young photographer—the pale one, as they called him—and let herself be tempted to go out for a walk in the woods after. And Thea, her sister, who was with them, had almost pinched her arm black and blue in her excitement. But it had to be; he was irresistible, with his foreign-looking appearance, his silver-mounted stick, and his smartly creaking calfskin boots.

He had not danced himself, by the way, but sat majestically apart drinking his tea.

But how he could talk! Until one hardly knew if it was real or all a dream....

It was light when she pulled off her soaking wet stockings and her sodden dancing shoes.

Yes, it must be some good angel that had put back the clock of time tonight. Here she was, walking in the woods of Aalborg with her lover. There was the fjord, and the moon drawing a silvery path right to her feet. Come, come!

She gazed with dimmed eyes towards the wondrous ball in the heavens, that called up tides in the seas and in hearts; she clung trustingly to her friend's arm. And, glancing at him sideways, she saw that his eyes were looking out towards it too. Yes, their glances moved together, taking the same road out over the gliding waters of the Belt, in through a gate of clouds, to kneel at the full moon, that is the God of Fools.

A startled bird rose at their feet and flew, the air rushing audibly in its feathers.

"Listen—a lark! And singing now, though it's night!"

"A lark!" Egholm took this, too, as an omen of good fortune for his turbine.

At the foot of the slope lay the boat, drawn up on land with props against the sides.

He explained it all, the parts that were there and the rest that should be added as soon as Krogh had got the turbine finished. He spoke eagerly and disconnectedly; none but an expert could have understood him. But Anna kept on saying:

"Yes, yes, I can understand that, of course. Ever so much better that way, yes. And how prettily it's painted, the boiler there. I thought it would be just an old rusty stove. And the boat—why, it's quite a ship in itself."

"Beautiful little boat, isn't it?" said Egholm, in high good humour now. "And I've caulked it all over. Take my word for it, the natives'll stare a bit when the day comes, and they see it racing away. Let's sit down and look at it a bit. Here, Anna, just here."

They sat down, but it was wet in the tufty grass.

"We can climb up in the boat and sit there."

Anna hesitated at first, but soon gave way. After all, everything was topsy-turvy already; she hardly knew if she were awake or dreaming. Egholm turned up an old bucket. "Here!" and he offered his hand like a polite cavalier and helped her up.

The summer night was all about them. The lapping of the waves sounded now near, now far; it was like delicate footsteps. For a little while neither spoke.

"But—you're not crying, Anna, dear?" He had felt her shoulders quivering.

"We've been so far away from each other; strangers like," she sniffed. And then she broke down completely. "Anna, dear," he had said. "Far away from each other.... I don't see how.... Seems to me we've been seeing each other all day the same as usual."

"Oh, but—we haven't talked together for an hour like we are now, not really, all the time we've been here."

"Well, what should we talk about? You don't generally take any interest in my things. And, besides, living as we do in a hell of poverty...."

"But that's just the reason why we ought to have helped each other. It would have made everything easier if we had."

"Well, I don't know…. But, anyhow, there's never been any difficulty on my part, I'm sure." Egholm spoke throughout with the same slight touch of surprise. Really, she was getting too unreasonable.

There was nothing for it now—she must say it.

"You've struck me many a time in the two years we've been living here." She stopped in fright at her own words, then hastened to add: "But I know you don't mean any harm, of course."

"Then why do you bother about it?" he said, in the same tone as before. But a moment later, before she could answer, he got up, reached out as if to swing himself out of the boat, then sat down again and shook his head.

"Struck you?" he said plaintively. "Have I really struck you?"

He did not expect an answer, but asked the same question again, all the same. He fumbled for her hand under her apron, and stroked it again and again.

"Have I really struck you?"

Then he drew back his hand again, and shook his head once more.

Anna was deeply moved. The single caress seemed to her like the sunlight and the scent of flowers that came in through the kitchen window in the morning, before the others were awake. Her heart swelled up within her, and her tears poured down as she put her arms round him and begged him to forget what she had said. She lost sight of the starting-point altogether, and behaved like a penitent sinner herself.

"Forgive me, do say you forgive me. Say you'll forget it. Oh, don't make me miserable now because it slipped out like that! You're so good, so good…."

White banks of mist lay over the Belt, and away in the north-east the sun was already preparing to emerge after the brief night. The larks rose and fell, singing; the gulls called cheerily as they came tearing down after food.

Egholm turned round several times to look back at the boat as they walked home.

Quietly they stole into the house. Nothing had gone wrong in their absence.

Hedvig awoke, and stared stiffly at her parents; then she yawned and lay down again. Very soon the chairs were rocking under her again as they should.

Egholm began undressing at once; he looked tired and peaceful. But his wife whispered to say she would be there directly; only a few more stitches to finish the work.

And as she sewed, she looked with a smile at the spots of red paint on her fingers. There, on the left hand, was one that looked just like a ring. That was where he had helped her up into the boat.

Who could sleep after a night like that?

XX

Draper Lund and Barber Trane came walking together from the direction of the town. Reaching Egholm's beach path, Lund broke off in the middle of a sentence, and said:

"Well, I think I'll go down this way. Enjoy the view, you know. Good-bye!"

"Why, I was going down that way myself. It's to-day that thing was to start, you know—the miracle man's steamboat thing."

"H'm. If it goes at all." Lund straightened his glasses and shot an unexpected glance of considerable meaning at the other.

"No, no, of course. But it's as well to know how it went off, you know, when customers come in and talk about it."

"I don't want to deliver any definite judgment," said Lund delicately, as a very Professor of Drapery, "but there is something about the man that leads me to doubt. He talks so much."

"Yes, and so mysterious about things. And conceited, too."

"Which, with his dirty vest and frayed trousers...." added Lund in agreement.

"I suppose he'll go sailing round with it to show it off?"

"I daresay he'll take out a patent."

"Those patent things are never any good," said Trane energetically. He knew. He had a patent pipe at home, that was always sour.

Lund and Trane stopped in surprise when they came down to the beach and found how many others of the townsfolk had had the same idea of going down that way. Lund made as if to turn back, but realised that it was too late, and laughed with great heartiness. And those on the spot laughed again in perfect comprehension—they had felt exactly the same way themselves. One of them had made a long detour round by Etatsraaden's garden, and others had done the same as Lund, walking smartly out as if going a long way, and then turning off suddenly, as if by the impulse of the moment, towards the beach.

Well, *Herregud!* here they were. And, anyhow, it was only reasonable to take what fun there might be going these sad times. There was not much in the way of amusement in the town.

Besides, it was pleasant enough, lying here in the soft dried seaweed and the warm tickling sand. The sun shone over the Belt and the green shores of Jutland beyond. They could, as Lund repeated again and again, enjoy the view.

He and Trane joined a group that had gathered for instruction in steam engines about the person of Lange, the schoolmaster.

"Then there's a pipe goes here...." The schoolmaster pointed to a certain spot in the air and came to a standstill. He was very nervous without a blackboard and his handbook of physics to help him out. And now here were those two unpleasant characters, Lund and Trane, lounging up in the middle of the lesson.

"A pipe goes there ... and that leads to the cylinder here...." He raised his voice and pointed again.

Trane, anxious to see as much as possible, craned his neck to follow the direction of Lange's index finger, but perceived, to his surprise, nothing more tangible than the driving clouds.

He shook his head. How could he tell his customers this? He gave it up, and lay down with the others to bask in the September sunshine.

Egholm's boat lay some twenty yards out; the shallow water prevented it from coming closer in. It was white, with a brilliant red stripe along the side. Behind the red-leaded funnel, which was supported with stays, could be seen curious parts of bright metal. Egholm was on his knees, hat in hand, puffing at the furnace. The fuel, which consisted of half-rotten fragments of board, was not quite dry. Now and again he lifted his head and gave a brief glance towards land.

Astonishing, such a lot of people had turned up. He felt his responsibility towards them like a delicious ache at his heart.

Oh, it would turn out all right.

If only he had had someone to lend a hand. Even Sivert would have been better than nothing. Egholm looked across reproachfully at Krogh, the old blacksmith, who stood on the beach with his jaws drooping as ever. He had just come down with the last bits of the machine, but could not be persuaded to go on board. He dared not mix with the rest, even, for he was an accomplice in the thing, however much he might turn up his nose to show disapproval.

Well, well, he would have to manage alone.

What was that?—who were they lifting their hats to suddenly?

Heavens, if it wasn't the editor himself! Egholm dropped a nut that slipped away between the bottom boards. Perhaps, after all, Anna had not been altogether lying when she said the editor had called him a genius. But he would not do discredit to the name—no, he would take care of that!

Trembling with emotion, Egholm watched the mighty personage striding through the groups. He always walked as if battling his way forward in the teeth of a gale. Even to-day, when the water was smooth as a mirror, his flowing cloak, his greyish-yellow military beard, even his bushy eyebrows, seemed to stand away from him as if borne on the wings of some private particular wind; possibly one he had brought home with him from the battlefields of '64.

The onlookers leaped aside, like recruits, to make way for him. His presence brought sudden encouragement to the rest—something would surely come of it, after all. A good thing they had not stayed at home.

The editor stopped at the water's edge, and hailed across, with a voice rent by the storm:

"Egholm! Can you get done by six, so that I can have a line in the paper?"

Egholm tried to rise, but slipped down again. He was rather cramped for room.

"I think so, yes, I think so!" He drew out his watch and looked at it. A quarter to nine it showed now—as it had done for heaven knows how long past. "I'll do my best."

The editor muttered something, balanced against a sudden gust, and marched off.

But there were plenty remaining. The slopes of the beach were alive and noisy as bird-cliffs in the nesting season.

How had all these people ever managed to find their way to the spot? Egholm had not drummed about any announcement as to time and place of his experiment. He had, indeed, grown rather more reticent of late. And old Krogh would hardly say more than he need. How could it have come about?

The explanation was there in the flesh—with a shawl about her head and beautifully varnished clogs on her feet. The explanation was Madam Hermansen, who had the backstairs entry of every house in Knarreby. Whatever was thrown into her as into a sink at one place was gladly used to wash up the coffee cups in at another. She smelt a little of everything, like a sewer, and was as useful and as indispensable.

In addition to this comprehensive occupation for the public weal, she found time to cherish great amorous passions for all the big fat men in the town. She walked about, smiling and confident, from group to group, shaking her hips at every step, and sidling round people like a horse preparing to kick.

"That leg of yours still bad?" asked little Dr. Hoff.

"Yes, much the same."

"H'm," said Hoff, a little annoyed. "Mind you keep it clean. That's the only thing to do."

"I suppose it's no use trying an earth cure?"

"Earth cure? What on earth's that?"

"Why, it's just an earth cure, that's all. It was Egholm's been plaguing me to try it. But he ... well, I'm not sure his intentions are really decent like and proper. I know how he's been with me sometimes ... and his poor wife...."

"What's he want you to do with the leg?" asked Hoff, his eyes glittering behind his glasses.

"Why, as sure as I'm alive, he wants me to bury it in the ground." Madam Hermansen laughed alarmingly.

"Now, does he mean? While it's on you, that is?" Hoff blinked again.

"Now, this moment, if he could get me to do it. And then sit there for a week, for the juices of the earth to work a cure, if you please."

"Well, mind you don't take root," said Hoff. His face was immobile, save for his eyes.

"What? Yes, and then all the worms and rats and things.... But how he can talk, that Egholm. Never knew such a man."

Wassermann from the Customs House came down too, his galoshes leaving a long dragging trail in the dry sand. Under the gold-braided cap his red wig stuck out, stiff as a tuft of hay. It was said he had inherited it from his father. Be that as it may, he certainly kept it in use, wore it at all times, and stayed religiously at home while it was being mended once a year by Fru Egholm. His features seemed erased, with the exception of his mouth, which appeared as a black cavity like a rat's hole in a white-washed wall. He stood for some minutes gaping over towards Egholm's boat, then he shambled on again. His moribund perceptions had had their touch of excitement, and that sufficed.

Henrik Vang had settled himself almost as in a cave, half-way up the slope between two willow bushes. Sivert, who had likewise succumbed to the prevalent fever, and run off from his glazier work in the middle of a day, had brought him down a whole case of beer. The boy had run so fast with the barrow that half the bottles were broken.

"No harm done as far as I'm concerned," said Vang solemnly as a funeral oration. "But it is a pity to waste good beer."

The onlookers of the better class came up to him one by one, to shake hands and dispose of a bottle of beer, as quietly as might be.

"Why the devil can't you come over to the rest of us?" said Rothe, who was dressed in his best, having just come from a meeting of the town council.

"Not such a fool. This is not the only place where there's any shade to cool the beer." Vang pointed under one of the bushes. "Look there—might be in the garden of Eden."

Henrik Vang himself was perspiring profusely, out of anxiety on his friend Egholm's behalf.

"Isn't it wonderful? Just look out there, and see it's really true. There's the boat—the steamer he's invented. Now, if I live to be a hundred"—here he glanced darkly at Rothe—"if I lived to be *two* hundred, I could never invent a steamboat. Not me."

"There've been steamboats before, I fancy," said Rothe.

"Eh, what?" Vang looked up sharply, and was for a moment at a loss; then he laughed, and waved Rothe aside with his broad paw. "Oh yes, those great big unwieldy things, I know. Any fool can make a thing like that. But a *little* steamboat—that's another thing!"

He caught sight of Sivert lying flat in the grass, dividing his attention equally between his father's manœuvres with the machinery and Vang's operations with the bottles.

"Come up here, boy!" cried Vang, and Sivert crawled nearer. He dared not let himself be seen, least of all by his father.

"How does he do it?" Vang looked sternly, but with unsteady gaze, at the boy. "You ought to know. How does your father manage it—inventing things and all that?"

"Like this!" said Sivert, without a moment's hesitation, shaking his woolly head from side to side like a rattle.

"The devil he does!"

"But it was me that invented the big brass tap in the cellar, though. But then it was a very little one, really. I don't think it was bigger than there to there," said Sivert modestly, indicating a length of Vang's leg from the ankle to the middle of the thigh. "Look how it's puffing now!"

The smoke was pouring out violently from the funnel of the boat, drifting in towards the onlookers as a foretaste of what was to come. Egholm was working away feverishly. Now he was seen clambering barefooted, with his trousers rolled up to the knee, out past the engine to the bow; a moment later, he was back in the stern, leaning over with his sleeves in the water up to the elbows, turning at the screw, or baling out water as frantically as if in peril of shipwreck.

Folk whispered to one another; now he was doing so-and-so....

But—what was this? Here was Egholm's girl Hedvig coming down, with the youngest child by the hand—what did she want? And wearing the famous button boots, too—the ones with ventilators in. Emanuel had one stocking hanging in rings about his ankle.

"What do *you* want?" Egholm's nose was smeared with soot and oil, and his brow was puckered angrily.

"There's a lady come to be taken."

"Tell her to come again to-morrow."

Egholm gave a single proud, firm glance towards the land. Then he bent down again over his spanner. The matter was decided. Hedvig tossed her head, fished up Emanuel out of the sand, and walked off.

What legs the girl had! But it was really indecent to go about like that, with her skirts cut short above the knee.

"Say your father's busy—dreadfully busy about something just now." Egholm consulted his dead watch once more. "Ask if she can't wait, say, about an hour, and I'll be there directly."

"Very well."

"Hedvig!" Egholm stood up and shouted. "Who was the lady?"

"A fine lady," said Hedvig, angry and ashamed.

"Ask her to sit down," said Egholm, his voice somewhat faint. "I'll come directly."

He thrust more fuel under the boiler, stepped over the side, and waded ashore, with his boots in his hand and his socks dangling out of his pockets.

"You're a smart one!" said Rothe, playfully threatening.

"Very annoying," said Egholm. "But I'll be back in five minutes' time."

He thrust his bare feet into his boots and ran up towards home.

"We may as well go," said Lange, the schoolmaster, looking round. "It won't come to anything, after all."

"I'm going out to have a look at the thing, anyhow," said Rothe, and began pulling off his boots.

"I'm half a mind to myself," said Dr. Hoff, tripping about.

"Give you a ride out, Doctor?" suggested Rothe.

Several of the onlookers laughed, but the little dark medico accepted the offer in all seriousness.

And suddenly quite a number decided to go out and look for themselves.

Trane, the barber, and schoolmaster Lange sat down back to back and began pulling off shoes and stockings. Lange put his hat over the foot he bared first.

"Ugh!" from one and then another as they dipped their feet. The water was cold.

"But surely—it looks like…." The Doctor stood in the boat, gazing nearsightedly at the engine. "Surely that's the lid of my old bathroom stove—you remember I sent it back to you?"

"Why, so it is!" cried Rothe. "Oho, so that was what he wanted the old scrap-iron for."

"Have you noticed the funnel?" said Lange.

All saw at once that the funnel was a milk-can with the button knocked out; the stays were made fast to the handles on either side. Lange laughed, with chattering teeth; it was abominably cold.

"It makes an excellent funnel, anyhow," said the Doctor shortly.

"Suppose the thing started off with us now," said Trane, measuring the distance to shore.

"We'd soon be at the bottom, in this rotten old hulk." Lange pointed to the water slopping about over the bottom boards. He had in his mind appointed Dr. Hoff head of the class, and did not care to address himself to others.

"No doubt," said Hoff sharply. "You'd have preferred him to start with mahogany and polished brass."

Lange turned away angrily; it was distressing to have to set a mental black mark against the name of his most promising pupil. But impertinence....

"Still, a man need not be stingy all round," said Trane. He was thinking of Egholm's bald pate and untouched beard, that rendered him independent of all the barbers in the world.

"Here, Rothe," said the Doctor. "Come and explain the thing. How's it supposed to work? I've seen plans and drawings of that sort, of course, but I don't mind admitting it's altogether beyond me."

"Oh," said Rothe, shrugging his shoulders and puckering his brows with a careless air, "it's not so easy to explain when you're not in the business. But, roughly, it's like this...." And he began setting forth briefly the principles of the turbine.

"And that, of course, can only go round one way. How he's ever managed to get it to reverse, the Lord only knows. There's nothing much to see from the outside."

"Well, we shall hear this evening how it works."

"Perhaps—perhaps not. I shouldn't be too certain. There's a heap of things to take into consideration, apart from what you might call the principle of the thing."

"How do you mean?"

"Well, you wouldn't see it, of course, but there's a hundred odd things. That boiler there, for instance—can he get up a sufficient head of steam with that? I don't believe it. A turbine wants any amount of steam to drive. If he got it fairly going, the thing'd simply burst. Hark! how it's thumping away already. But there's no danger as long as he's only got that dolls' house grate to heat it with. And as for the boat"—Rothe looked round to make sure that Lange was out of hearing; the others were limping back shiveringly to land —"the freckle-nosed birch-and-ruler merchant's right enough; it's simply falling to pieces as it is. Egholm, poor devil, he got some odd bits of tin from my place and patched up the worst parts, but the nails wouldn't hold even then.—Coming off, Doctor? Here, get up again.—And the stuff he's burning's no better than hay. He's been stoking away for a couple of hours now, and hasn't got up steam yet."

"What d'you reckon it would cost to make the experiment properly?" asked the Doctor, with his expressionless face, as they reached dry land again.

"Oh, any amount of money. Thousands of *kroner*. It's hopeless for a poor devil like him to try. But, of course, once he could get the thing to go once round and reverse, why, *he'd be a millionaire!*"

Rothe shouted out the last words to the whole assembly; then he hopped across to Henrik Vang's bush. He pricked up his ears at the murmur that arose from his words.

Madam Hermansen had only just discovered Vang. Suddenly she stood at the foot of the slope and gave an amorous laugh.

Vang took the bottle from his lips in the middle of a draught, and the beer frothed over down his vest.

"Get out!" he cried, with horror in his face. "Get out!" And he threw the bottle at her.

Vang was a big man among his fellows; but under Madam Hermansen's glance he felt himself naked and ashamed.

Madam Hermansen sidled away in her polished clogs, still smiling.

Egholm came back at a trot, pushing an old perambulator full of coals. He breathed in relief to find that the crowd was still there; it had, indeed, increased. The workmen from the factory had come down to the beach on their way home, and stood there now talking in bass voices, their eyes turning ridiculously in their black faces. The apprentice lads had come, too—unable to resist. They felt a kind of primitive, brutally affectionate attraction towards the boat, which for some unexplained reason they had christened *The Long Dragon*. It was just the right distance for a stone-throwing target, and gave a delightful metallic sound when hit. They had used it as a bathing-station while the weather was still warm, undressing in it, diving in from it, and rocking it in the water till the waves washed up on the sand. They heaved up the anchoring stones, and sailed out with it, shouting and singing, into deep water, where they swam round it in flocks, like grampus about a whale. They turned the screw and made bonfires under the boiler. But they did more: they laid an oar across from gunwale to gunwale, and danced on it to see if it would break. And found it did. They threw the manometer into the water to see if it would float. And found it didn't. A pale youngster, the son of Worms, the brewer, who was not a factory apprentice at all, but a fine gentleman in the uniform of the Academy, found a pot of paint under one of the seats, and promptly painted his name, *Cornelius*, in red on the side of the boat.

This was not done merely in jest, but by way of revenge for a nasty jagged cut he had sustained when making his first investigations.

Egholm waged a continual hopeless war against those boys. It was rarely that he encountered them himself, but he found their traces frequently. When he did happen to catch one, it always turned out to be an innocent, who did not even know the others of the band.

This evening, however, in the presence of so many respectable citizens, the boys stood with hunched-up shoulders and hands in their pockets, silent, or speaking only in whispers. Now and again they nudged one another, like owls on a beam in the church tower.

The fire was being fed properly now, with coal, sending out a cloud of smoke like a waving velvet banner. There was a rasp of filing and sharp strokes of a hammer; the sound of iron against iron. Then down came a compositor boy with the editor's compliments, and....

"You can tell him I guarantee the machine will work all right. I *guarantee* it—you understand. And...."

"Then it hasn't gone yet?"

"But you can see for yourself," cried Egholm in despair; "the pressure's there all right now." And, to prove it, he sprang up and pulled at the little steam whistle. It gave a shriek as if to call for help—then died away.

"Hark at the cock-crow!" shouted Sivert, beside himself. "The world-famous cock crowing."

"What's that he's shouting about?"

No one had understood the words. But they saw the boy dancing on the crest of a hill with his white curls whirling about his head, and the enthusiasm laid hold on them, too. They leaped up from their mounds of seaweed, and in the dusk it seemed to them as if the boat moved. There was a tickling in their throats. Vang was weeping copiously already.

"Give him a cheer," said the doctor, moving from group to group. The doctor with his glasses was not to be contradicted.

They filled their lungs with air ready for a shout; then up came Petrea Bisserup, dragging her father along, and that air was expended in laughter.

Bisserup was a blind brushmaker, who lived in a little white house on the outskirts of the town. He was a little grey man, with a felt hat several sizes too large, and his face so covered with a fungus-growth of beard that only his nose showed through. His daughter, who led him, had a crooked neck, which bent over so far as to leave her head lying archly on one shoulder; she was a woman grown, but wore short skirts and cloth shoes. They were a remarkable pair, and in face of this counter-attraction, Egholm's wonder-boat might have sailed away to Jutland without being noticed by the crowd.

"Ei, ei…. Anything hereabout for a blind man to see?"

The boys from the factory could contain themselves no longer; one of them barged another over against the old man, while the rest chuckled and cackled and quacked like a yard full of mixed poultry.

"Petrea—here, Petrea, what are you looking at?"

"Little devils!" said Trane, gloating over them all the same. Lund, the scientific draper, laughed too, but schoolmaster Lange, recollecting his lessons at the drawing school, shrank back a little.

Petrea strode untroubled through the crowd, her mouth hanging open, and the old man trailing behind at her skirts like some uncouth goblin child. His moleskin breeches were of enormous capacity; the seat hung down behind to his calves. When he stood still, the superfluous folds fluttered in the wind like a rag-and-patch tent at a fair.

"Is't that way there, Petrea?" He pointed with his stick, and leant over, listening.

It was growing dusk. Folk were beginning to shiver a little in the evening air. And there was nothing amusing after all in the sight of these two poor vagrants. What was the time?

When Egholm opened the furnace door, the column of smoke shone like gold, and his face glowed fantastically big and red. Still a few more degrees were needed on the manometer—just a few. He stoked away, till the sparks flew like shooting stars across the sky. A fever seized him; he threw on coal with his bare hands, and found himself grasping with all ten fingers at a single lump.

Every second he glanced over at the shore, though it was impossible to distinguish anything clearly now.

Trembling, he heard a burst of laughter, that rolled like a wave along the line.

"Look straight ahead, Petrea, pretty Petrea, do!"

Heaven be thanked—they were not laughing at him, after all. If only the coals had been a little better. But it was dust and refuse, every handful.

"Is Dr. Hoff here?" someone cried.

"Who's asking for *me*?"

"There's a cart from the country."

The doctor cast a final glance at the water, where the glow from the fire played like a shoal of red fish; then he walked away with little hurried steps.

"I'm off," said Lange. "I don't see what there is to stand about here for."

What was there to stand about there for? No one could find any satisfactory answer.

It was dark and cold, and wife and supper were waiting at home.

The crowd broke up in little groups by common instinct. Lund and Trane went. The workmen from the factory went. All of them together.

Over between the two bushes Rothe was giving orders in a low voice. It was Henrik Vang being lifted on to a wheelbarrow. Sivert and his bosom friend, Ditlev Pløk, the cobbler's boy, were hauling each at one leg. When they came up to the level road, Sivert left the work to Ditlev, and clambered up himself beside Vang. The boy was wild with delight, and bubbling over with laughter and snatches of song. Madam Hermansen hurried up after them.

What had they been thinking of?

Away, away! homeward; see, the lights were lit already in the town.

The factory boys whistled like rockets, and marched in procession two and two about Petrea and her father.

The respectable citizens stepped out briskly to get warm, and laughed modestly one to another, like peasants emerging from a conjurer's tent.

But never again!

The sound of footsteps died away on the path, and the last of the figures disappeared into the gloom, leaving a solitary figure still waiting on the beach —a little woman, shivering under a white knitted kerchief. It was Fru Egholm. No one had seen her come; she sat as if under a spell, watching the myriad sparks that rose in curves against the evening sky, to fall and expire in the sand.

XXI

A few weeks have passed. It is just after dawn.

Up on the beach, Egholm and Sivert are toiling away till their feet are buried in the sand, hauling away at a rope that runs through a square-cut block to the boat. They bend forward and tug till their faces are fiery red. Then at last the *Long Dragon* yields and scrapes slowly up over the stones on to the sand. There it lies, like a newly caught fish, with a growth of shell and weed under its belly.

"Now—up with her! Put your shoulder to it, slave! That's it! Now up and bale her out."

Sivert had discovered that the water drained out of the boat from one of the tin patches, and found therefore no need to hurry, but followed with greater interest his father's operations. Egholm clambered up the slope, vanished between two bushes, and came down again laden with a sack bigger than himself. It was evidently light in proportion to its bulk, since it could be carried by one hand. In the other he held a bottle.

Up to now, Sivert had seen only his father's usual harsh look, but as he came down to the boat this time his expression changed to a great smile.

"Now for a grand burnt-offering, boy! The biggest that ever was since the days of Abraham and Isaac. No; stay where you are. I'm not going to sacrifice you; *that* wouldn't be much of a sacrifice, anyway. It's the boat—the turbine. Bale away; we must have it thoroughly dry."

Sivert splashed about with the dipper, and his father, still smiling, opened the sack. It was full of shavings.

"A sacrifice and a burnt-offering to the Lord."

"Wouldn't it work, then—the brass tap?"

"The turbine, you mean? Work and work, why...." Egholm shrugged his shoulders. "Oh yes, it worked all right. *My* calculations were right enough. Couldn't be wrong. But *the Lord* wouldn't have it. Didn't suit Him to let my little invention come out just now, and so"—again a mighty shrug of the shoulders—"so, of course, I gave it up. I think she'll do now."

He began tearing out handfuls of shavings and spreading them over the boat fore and aft; they filled up beautifully now they were loose.

"No," he went on; "God wouldn't have it. I felt it while I was stoking the fire that day. The pressure wouldn't come as it should, though I'd brought down a whole perambulator full of coal. Then at last, when He sent away the crowd that had come to see, I understood—I understood that He was jealous of my triumph and wouldn't have it. Well, He can have it now."

Sivert kept carefully to the opposite side of the boat, away from his father. It was safer, he felt, in case.... For, despite the smile, it was evident that his father was in a highly excited state. He did not scruple to walk round from one side to the other through the water, with his boots and socks on, though the waves splashed up over his knees. Sivert felt it would have been better to go round the other end of the boat, on dry land. At any rate, he preferred that way himself.

Now for the bottle. Egholm waved it generously, sprinkling the paraffin over the shavings and woodwork. Sivert, too, began to find it amusing. Paraffin and shavings—that was the thing!

"Got a match?"

Had he not! Sivert's fingers had been itching for minutes past to get at the box.

"Right—then fire away!"

Sivert struck a light, but the wind blew it out at once. He took a whole bundle in his fingers, leaned in over the edge of the boat, and struck. They went off like tiny shells, sputtering out on every side, but the shavings remained as dead as the sand of the beach. Once more he tried the same way, and this time it seemed with better success. There was a glow deep down among the mass. But nothing came of it save a smouldering redness that sent a thin white smoke out over the side. The lowest layer of shavings must have been wetted by the water in the bottom.

Egholm fired up in sudden anger.

"Get out of it, you Cain! Spoiling my burnt-offering!" He grasped an oar and struck out at the boy.

Sivert slipped aside unscathed, and clambered up to the top of the slope.

With a couple of furious blows, Egholm struck the oar through the rotten planks. The wind rushed in through the opening, and next moment a burst of flame rose several feet into the air.

A ship laden with flames!

Egholm stood as if petrified; then he began hurriedly throwing on more combustibles. He had a tar barrel and another huge sack of shavings, besides a whole pile of dry driftwood.

The funnel stays burned through, and the funnel blew off as a hat is torn from a man's head.

The tar barrel lay on a thwart, spewing green flame from its mouth. The sides had caught already. Egholm took up an armful of crackling dry weed and threw it in. As he did so, he happened to catch sight of the little manometer, and he sprang back in dismay. The indicator had worked round as far as it could, and stood firmly pressed against the stopping-pin.

God in Heaven! He had forgotten the water in the boiler! Another second and it would burst!

True, that mattered little, since the boat and all its contents were to be sacrificed. Nevertheless, Egholm picked up the oar and thrust it here and there among the flames, trying to open some valve or other. He had not reckoned on a bursting boiler, which would be out of place, to say the least, in a burnt-offering. He flung his coat about his face to shield him from the flames, and stabbed blindly with his oar.

Suddenly the burning boat seemed to shiver. Egholm dropped his oar and sprang back, expecting to see the whole thing explode....

When he turned round, he saw a strange sight. The screw was revolving at a furious rate, just touching the surface, and flinging up a hail of salt water against the wind.

He stooped forward, bending low down, his mouth agape with overwhelming astonishment. This was more of a marvel than anything he had seen. He had lied when he said the thing had worked all right the first time. At any rate, he knew nothing of how it had worked himself. He had simply had some parts made according to his own idea, and screwed them together. Now, he could hear the turbine whirring round, saying dut-dut, just as he had dreamed.

It only remained to see if it would reverse. Could he reverse the steering-gear in all that flame and smoke? It would have to be done swiftly—swiftly—for in a moment the boiler would be empty.

He worked and wriggled away with the oar, unheeding the fire that singed his beard and eyebrows. When this proved fruitless, he wrapped wet seaweed thickly round his arm and thrust it into the flames.

He had found it now, though in agonising pain. Then—the screw stood still a moment, and whirled round the opposite way. Egholm could feel the water spurting up towards him now. It soothed his burns. He stood still, close up to the boat, and wept.

Sivert sat up on the slope, watching it all. His father called to him to come down.

"D'you see that?" he cried. Despite the grime and the red burns, his face wore a look of supreme exaltation. "D'you see that?"

"She's puffing away finely," Sivert admitted.

Just then something snapped inside, and the engine stopped. Egholm ran for more weed to wrap round his arm, but, before he was ready, the explosion came. The sound was scarcely heard in the gale, only a slight *pouf*, but it split the boat lengthways like a ripe pea-pod.

Egholm looked on, delighted.

"D'you know what I think?" he said, cooling his martyred hand. "I think, my boy, we've done a great thing to-day. We've made a great burnt-offering unto the Lord. But more than that. We've—yes, in a way, *we've heaped coals of fire on His head!*"